THE
POLISH BOXER

Eduardo Halfon

*translated by Daniel Hahn, Ollie Brock,
Lisa Dillman, Thomas Bunstead,
and Anne McLean*

BELLEVUE LITERARY PRESS
NEW YORK

First Published in the United States in 2012 by
Bellevue Literary Press, New York

FOR INFORMATION CONTACT:
Bellevue Literary Press
NYU School of Medicine
350 First Avenue
OBV A612
New York, NY 10016

The Polish Boxer first appeared in Spanish as
El boxeador polaco, Copyright © 2008 by Editorial Pre-Textos
An earlier version of this translation of "Distant" was first published in
The Iowa Review, volume 41, number 2.

The publisher would like to thank Mary Bisbee Beek, Jesus Martin-Basas,
and Words Without Borders for helping to bring this book to
English-speaking readers.

Library of Congress Cataloging-in-Publication Data
Halfon, Eduardo, 1971-
 [Boxeador polaco. English]
 The Polish boxer / Eduardo Halfon ; translated by Daniel Hahn, Ollie
Brock, Lisa Dillman, Thomas Bunstead, and Anne McLean. — 1st ed.
   p. cm.
 ISBN 978-1-934137-53-6 (pbk. : alk. paper)
 I. Hahn, Daniel. II. Title.
 PQ7499.3.H35B6913 2012
 863'.7--dc23

                              2012016416

Bellevue Literary Press would like to thank all its generous
donors—individuals and foundations—for their support.

 This publication is made possible by the New York State Council on the
Arts with the support of Governor Andrew Cuomo and the New York
NYSCA State Legislature.

Book design and composition by Mulberry Tree Press, Inc.
Manufactured in the United States of America.

FIRST EDITION

1 3 5 7 9 8 6 4 2

ISBN 978-1-934137-53-6

THE
POLISH BOXER

I have moved the typewriter into the next room where I can see myself in the mirror as I write.

—HENRY MILLER

THE
POLISH BOXER

Distant

I was pacing among them, moving up and down between the rows of desks as if trying to find my way out of a labyrinth. We were reading from a Ricardo Piglia essay. We read about the dual nature of the short story, and it didn't surprise me, as I looked out, to be met with a sea of faces covered in acne and heartfelt bewilderment. We read that a story always tells two stories. We read that the visible narrative always hides a secret tale. The story's construction makes something hidden appear artificially, we read, and then I asked them if they'd understood it, any of it, but it was as though I were speaking some Bantu language. Silence. But rashly, undaunted, I stepped further into the labyrinth. Several of them were dozing. Others were doodling. An overly thin girl toyed with her long blond locks, absent-mindedly coiling and uncoiling a twist of hair around an index finger. Beside her, a pretty-boy eyed her lasciviously. And from within that vast silence, I heard the drone of tittering and whispering and gum chewing and then, as I did every year, I asked myself if this shit was really worth it.

I don't know what I was doing trying to teach literature to a horde of college kids who were, for the most part, illiterate. Each fall, they'd register for their first year, still emanating a sort of doleful puppy-dog air. Looking like lost sheep, yet smugly convinced that they weren't, that they knew everything there was to know, that they possessed the most absolute understanding of the secrets governing the universe. Who cared about literature? Who cared about one more course with one more stupid jackass spouting even more stupid bullshit about books, and oh books are so wonderful, and books are so important, yeah, whatever, dream on, but me, I'm fine with no books and no jackass who still thinks literature matters. They were thinking something like that, I suppose. And I suppose, too, that seeing them sit there year after year with those same self-satisfied expressions, those haughty yet ignorant looks on their faces, I understood them perfectly, and even almost conceded their point, and recognized in them some trace of myself.

It's like the stars.

I turned around and saw a thin, dark-skinned kid whose fragile features made me think for some reason of a rosebush—not a rosebush in bloom, but a sad, spindly rosebush with not a single rose on it. Several students giggled.

Excuse me?

It's like the stars, he said again, softly. I asked him his name. Juan Kalel, he replied just as quietly, without looking at me. I asked him to explain what he meant by that, and he sat in silence for a moment, as if ordering his thoughts. Well, stars are stars, he said timidly, and again came the tittering, but I asked him to please continue. I mean, the stars in the sky are the stars that we see, but they're also something more, something that we can't see but that's still there. I said nothing, giving him space, giving him time to elaborate. If we arrange them, they become constellations, he murmured, which represent zodiac signs, which in turn represent each one of us. I replied that was all well and good, but what did it have to do with a story? He was silent again, and while he thought, I sauntered back to the desk where I'd left my milky coffee and took a long, tepid sip. What I mean is, he continued falteringly, as if each word pained him, a story is something we see, something we read, but if we arrange it, it becomes something else too, something we can't see but that's still there, between the lines, implicit.

The other students sat in silence, staring at Juan Kalel as though he were a freak, awaiting my reaction. I considered the metaphysical and aesthetic ramifications of his words, the many implications that even Juan Kalel himself probably wasn't aware of. But I made no comment. Instead, between sips of coffee, I simply smiled at him.

After class, back in the faculty lounge, I poured more coffee into my paper cup, lit a cigarette, and began leafing distractedly through the newspaper. A psychology professor, a woman by the name of Gómez or González or something, sat down beside me and asked what class I was teaching. Literature, I said. Wow, tough, she replied, though I have no idea why. She wore too much makeup and her hair was dyed a weary shade of ocher, the color of a kinkajou or an abandoned doll. The rim of her cup was already kiss-marked red. And what are the kiddies reading? she asked a bit too jovially. She actually called them kiddies. I stared at her with as much solemnity and intolerance as I could muster and, exhaling a cloud of smoke, told her that for now we were doing a few Donald Duck and Pluto stories. Well, she said, and that was all she said.

I spent the next few days thinking about Juan Kalel. I'd managed to find out that he was on a full scholarship, in his first year, and majoring in economics. He was seventeen years old and a native of Tecpán, a beautiful city of artichokes and fir trees in Guatemala's western altiplano region, though calling it a city might be a bit of a stretch and calling them fir trees might be a bit optimistic. Everything about Juan Kalel was out of sync with the other students in my class and, of course, the whole university. His sensitivity and eloquence. His interest. His appearance and social status.

As is the case at many private Latin American universities, the vast majority of students from Francisco Marroquín University come from wealthy families, or families who think they're wealthy and therefore also think they've got their children's economic futures all sewn up. As a consequence, their degrees become mere trinkets, awarded to prove that some family custom or other has been followed, and to stifle gossip. In fact, you could easily claim that the disdainful, pedantic attitude you see there is actually more pronounced in the first-year students whom I, with unmistakable fatigue, had to accept into my classes each year. I'm generalizing, and perhaps recklessly, but the world can only be understood through generalizations.

From time to time, however, out of that great mass of falsehood and hypocrisy, there appears (to expand on his metaphor) a shooting star like Juan Kalel, who has vocation and devotion and a passion for all types of learning, which stems from a genuine need and not some pathetic and deplorable sophism, and who, by saying a few words, exposes the falsehood and hypocrisy not just of the other students, but sometimes even of the professor and his stuffy ivory tower.

The first author on the syllabus was Edgar Allan Poe, a logical jumping-off point, I think, given that it was a contemporary short story course. I'd asked them to read two of his stories, "The Purloined Letter" and "The Black Cat," thereby enabling us to cover his detective stories with one and suspense fiction with the other.

At the beginning of class, a pudgy girl raised her hand and said she hadn't liked the stories at all. Fine, I said, that's your right, but tell us why. To which she simply replied, making a disgusted face: Just really gross. A few people laughed; others seconded her opinion. Yeah, really gross. So I explained to them that taste has to be accompanied by a more refined understanding, that most of the time we dislike something simply because we don't understand it, haven't really made an effort to understand it, and the easiest response is just to claim we haven't liked it and wash our hands of the whole affair. You've got to develop criteria, I said, exercise your ability to analyze and synthesize, and not just spit out empty opinions. You've got to learn to read past the words, I said, rather poetically, I believe, though no doubt all I did was confuse them further. I spent the rest of the period fleshing out the intricacies of both stories, the almost invisible network of symbolism Poe had cast just beneath the surface of each text like a supporting framework.

Any questions? I asked after wrapping up. And a boy with long hair asked, as someone does each year, if authors like Poe did that on purpose, like, wove a second story line, a secret narrative into the gaps in the visible one, or if it just came out spontaneously. And as I did every year, I said that you'd have to ask him, but that in my opinion, therein lay the difference between a writer and a great writer: the ability to be saying one thing when in reality you were expressing another, the ability to use language as a means of accessing a sublime, ephemeral metalanguage. Like a ventriloquist? he asked. Yes, I suppose so, I said, although later, when I gave it some more thought, I regretted having said it.

After class, the pudgy girl came up as I was gathering my things. I still don't like the stories, she said. I smiled and asked her her name. Ligia Martínez. That's all right, Ligia, neither Poe nor I are offended. But I will say, professor, that I understand them better now, and I reproached her for calling me professor. I'm sorry, doctor, she said, and I chided her again. He doesn't like to be called doctor or professor, said a girl waiting for her by the exit, someone I hadn't seen before. What should I call you, then? Ligia asked. Just call him Eduardo, the other girl said with a slight smile, and I saw that she had eyes the color of molasses, or at least that's how they looked to me at that moment, in that light. So listen, Ligia said, I wanted to ask you why there aren't more women writers on the syllabus. There's only one, Eduardo, this O'Conolly or whatever. Doesn't that seem, like, politically incorrect? she asked with a hint of malice. And I gave her the same reply I give every year. There are also no black writers, Ligia, or Asian writers, or midget writers, and as far as I'm aware, there's only one gay writer. I told her that my courses were politically incorrect, thank God. In other words, Ligia, they're honest. Just like art. Great short story writers, period. She said fine, that she was just curious, and left with her friend.

Juan Kalel was waiting for me outside class, leaning against the wall, alone. Do you have a minute, Halfon? he asked, pronouncing my last name in a very odd way, as if it were somehow stressed on both syllables. I said of course I did, and then I said I was surprised at how silent he'd been in class. I wanted to speak to you, he said, ignoring my comment and staring down at the ground. I saw then that he had an enormous purple scar on his right cheek. Like he'd been whacked with a machete, I thought. And then I thought briefly of the white pockmarks on that black wall at Auschwitz that my Polish grandfather had told me about. Juan took a folded-up piece of paper out of his shirt pocket and handed it to me. It's a poem, Halfon. I asked him if he wanted me to read it right then, and he said no, startled, backing up a couple of steps, later, please, whenever you have a little time. I'd be happy to, Juan, and I was going to shake his hand, but he kept backing up, slowly, as he proffered thanks without ever looking at me.

They read Maupassant's "The Horla."

Before I began, I asked all those who hadn't liked the story to put up their hands. Six hands rose timidly. Then seven. Eight. All right, you eight come up to the front of the class, I said, and they sauntered casually up to the front of the group until at last they formed a sort of crooked line of suspects. Tell us what you didn't like about it. First one: I don't know. Second: Well, I didn't finish it, so I just didn't like it. Third: It's totally impossible to understand, the author doesn't make any sense, and I don't like people who don't make sense. Fourth: Too long. Fifth: Too long. (Laughter.) Sixth: I felt sorry for the crazy guy. Seventh: I only like positive stories, stories that inspire me and make me want to live, not just depress me. Eighth: Yeah, same here, it made me feel bad, and who wants to feel bad? I remained silent, glancing from them to the rest of the class, trying to let something sink in without my having to say it outright. Not a chance. So I thanked them, told them they could sit down, and slowly proceeded to analyze the story, point out the most important elements and recurring themes, the many phrases that were like beautiful doors leading into a secret story. A difficult read, elliptical, perhaps incomprehensible, but magisterial nonetheless.

See you next week, I said when I'd finished. Señor Kalel, would you stay behind, please? And after answering a few individual questions from other students and gathering my things, I asked Juan to go with me to have a cigarette in the cafeteria. He just nodded. A man of few words, Juan Kalel.

We walked in silence, a pleasant silence, natural, like in a silent movie when it's not actually silence but just the normal state of affairs. I bought two coffees and then we went and sat down at the farthest table. I lit a cigarette. Maupassant's really good, Juan whispered as I stirred in my sugar. An architecture professor walked over to say hello, but I didn't stand, so he left right away. Juan had burned his mouth on the coffee and was gingerly fingering his lips. I really like that image of the stalk bent by an invisible hand, he said with such overwhelming sadness that I thought he might be on the verge of tears. Me too, though I'm not sure why, I replied, reaching for the ashtray. So, Juan, I read your poem, and then I stopped and took tiny sips of my coffee. He was still blowing into his. I told him it was really quite good. Juan looked up and said he knew. We both smiled. I bit down lightly on my cigarette so that I could pull the poem from the pocket of my green leather bag, and then reread it in silence. What about the title? I asked. It doesn't have one, he replied, I don't believe in titles. They're a necessary evil, Juan. Maybe, but I still don't believe in them. He paused. Like you, Halfon, he added with a wry smile, you don't seem to believe in personal titles. Touché, señor, I replied, and as I stubbed out my cigarette, I asked him if he had other poems, if he'd written any more. He was still blowing into his coffee. Without looking up, he told me he'd written that one in my class the other day, while I was discussing Poe's stories. He said he wrote poems whenever he felt something very strongly, no matter where he was, although the poem was always about something very different from what he was feeling. He said he had notebooks full of poems at home. He said I was the first person to read one.

Two days later, I got an e-mail from the girl with molasses eyes. Her name was Ana María Castillo, but she signed off with a syrupy Annie. Immediately I pictured the red-headed orphan with ringlets, even though this girl was tall and pale, with straight hair, astonishingly shoe-polish black.

Her note was short and, to my surprise, flawlessly composed. In it, she said that she hadn't liked the Maupassant story either, but that she'd been ashamed to admit it in front of the class. That's why I'm writing, she said. To explain why I didn't like it. First, I want you to know that I read it twice, just as you say we should, and that I understood it, or at least part of it. But that's not why I didn't like it. The reason I didn't like it is because I identified so strongly with the protagonist. Sometimes I feel that lonely too, and I don't know what to do about it, how to handle it. I guess we hate seeing what we really are.

I replied to her that same night, and the tone of my e-mail was more petulant than I'd realized. Congratulations, I wrote. That's the correct way to read a story: letting yourself be dragged along in the author's wake. It matters not whether the waters are calm or stormy. What counts is having the courage and confidence to dive in headfirst. And that's when literature, and art in general, becomes a sort of mirror, Annie, a mirror in which all of our perfections and imperfections are reflected. And, yes, some of them are frightening. Others are painful. Fiction is funny that way, isn't it? A story is nothing but a lie. An illusion. And that illusion only works if we trust in it. The same way a magic trick impresses us even though we know perfectly well that it's a trick. The rabbit doesn't actually disappear. The woman hasn't actually been sawed in half. But we believe it. The illusion is real, oxymoronically. Plato wrote that literature is a deceit in which he who deceives is more honest than he who does not deceive, and he who allows himself to be deceived is wiser than he who does not.

Next came Chekhov. They read three relatively short stories and I gathered no one understood a word. Or maybe no one read them. Frustrated, I gave them a test for the remainder of the period, and sat before them enthralled, reading one of Juan Kalel's notebooks.

After class, Juan was there when I left, leaning against the wall again, waiting for me. We walked to the cafeteria, and this time he insisted on buying the coffee. I thanked him. Once we'd sat down, I pulled out his notebook and placed it on the table and lit a cigarette. I asked him what he was doing studying economics, but he just shrugged, and we both knew it was a ridiculous question. What does your family do in Tecpán? My father tends an orchard in Pamanzana, just outside of Tecpán, he said, and my mother works in a textile factory. No siblings? Three sisters, all younger. He told me his scholarship covered housing too, paying for a room in a student residence in the city. What about you, Halfon, why did you study engineering? Because I was a fool, I said, and then we sat in silence for a few minutes, drinking coffee while I smoked and wondered about his family life. He was incongruous, Juan Kalel. Sometimes he seemed to radiate the most absolute innocence, an utter naïveté, as genuine and obvious as the scar on his cheek. But other times he gave the impression of understanding everything, of having lived and suffered through things that most of us come to know only through reading or supposition or puerile theories. Without smiling, he seemed always to be smiling, and without crying, he seemed to have indelible tears on his cheeks. I asked him who his favorite poets were and he said Rimbaud and Pessoa and Rilke. Especially Rilke, he said. I don't see much Rilke in your poems, Juan, or at least not in the ones I've read so far. Rilke is in all of my poems, he said, and

I didn't ask him why, although much later I would come to understand perfectly. You don't write poetry? he asked. Never, I said, stubbing out my cigarette, and I was going to say that I didn't consider myself a poet, that in my opinion, to be a poet you have to believe you are one, be born one, whereas a prose writer can slowly evolve—but in the end I didn't manage to say anything at all. Someone greeted me from behind, and when I turned, I found myself looking into Annie Castillo's molasses eyes, which is simply a figure of speech, because the only thing molasses about them was a mistaken memory. Still, I stood up.

How are you, Eduardo? She was clasping her books to her chest, like a life vest, I thought, and she asked if we were busy. I said we were, a little. Oh well, I just wanted to thank you in person for answering my e-mail. No need, Annie. And to say that maybe one day, if you're free, we could meet up and talk, she murmured, blushing. I said of course, I'd love to, and she smiled nervously. Let's arrange a time by e-mail, then, she said, holding out a hand that was long and thin and far too cold.

After I sat back down, I lit another cigarette and noticed that as Annie walked away, Juan Kalel seemed particularly focused as he gazed at her ass.

Nothing happens in this story, declared an emaciated boy whose last name was Arreola. What, so some guy has a few drinks with an old friend and then he goes home. I mean, what's so great about that? he scoffed, same thing I do every Friday. A few students laughed awkwardly.

I told them Joyce had to be read much more carefully.

They had to know a little about the history of Ireland, the religious conflict. They had to grasp the context of each story, its structure and rich symbolism. But more than anything, they had to get a feel for his epiphanies.

Anyone know what epiphany means? A cat-like girl said it was sort of like the epiphany of Jesus. Pretty much, but what does that mean? Oh, I don't remember, she said. All right, pay attention. Rustling of papers, readying of pencils. In Greek theater, the epiphany is the moment when a god appears to impose order on the scene. In the Christian tradition, the Epiphany refers to the revelation of Jesus' divinity to the Magi. So, it's a moment of clarity. And in the Joycean sense, an epiphany is an unexpected revelation had by one of his characters. A sudden spiritual manifestation, as he himself called it. I enunciated slowly. Does everyone get that? Absolute silence, which of course meant no.

Let's start with the title. In Spanish, it's called "Una nubecilla"—a small cloud, almost a cloudlet—but that's a terrible translation, I said. None of the story's Spanish translators, including the great Cuban writer Cabrera Infante, did a good job on that. The original title is "A Little Cloud," which we know Joyce took from the Bible, Book of Kings. Anybody remember what happened in the Book of Kings? One girl started to say something and then faltered, stopped. I explained in very general terms that the people of Israel had been led away from God. Elijah prophesied a drought that would last until the people stopped worshiping false prophets and returned to Jehovah. And after two years without so much as a drop of rain, after the fall of Ahab and the false prophets, the people of Israel returned to God, and Elijah's servant proclaimed: Behold, there ariseth a little cloud out of the sea, like a man's hand. In other words, ladies and gentlemen: Watch out, it's about to rain. Think about it. Not a small cloud, but a little cloud. Why is that distinction so important in the context of the story? Pause. Why am I insisting that Cabrera Infante and company not only did a poor job translating the title, but actually translated it in a way that leads the reader astray, further from what the story really means?

Juan Kalel raised his hand and said that there could be some sort of relation between the optimism of the approaching cloud in the Bible and the false optimism of Chico Chandler, as he was called in Spanish. Because in English, he continued, it would be Little Chandler and Little Cloud, right? Which in Spanish should have been Pequeño Chandler and Pequeña Nube. The repetition draws a parallel that we miss in the Spanish, he said. Quite pleased, I walked back to the desk for my coffee. What I mean is, Juan went on, Chandler is all talk. He talks about all the things he's going to do, all the poems he's going to write, and how one day he's going to get out of Dublin, too, and live as free and fully as his friend Gallagher. But then when he gets home all he can do is yell at his son and make him cry. It's sort of pathetic. And ironic too. The relationship between the story's two littles, the cloud and Chandler, is ironic, because it's obvious that he's never going to do the things he wants to do. Unlike the biblical cloud, he's hopeless. It's as though he's paralyzed, Juan said, gazing at me absently, as if something much more personal, but equally unattainable, had dawned on him.

Smiling, I asked them if they'd understood. Annie Cassaised her hand. Well, I think there's something more to it, she murmured. I said that there was, that of course there was something more. I mean, she began, I don't know, but I don't think the irony in the title is gratuitous. And then she fell silent. Precisely, I replied, but why not? Why isn't it? What other irony do we get a glimpse of in the story, Annie? But she simply shook her head and shrugged. I turned to Juan, hoping to prod him into bailing her out, but he was engrossed in his notebook, scribbling furiously. A poem, perhaps. I don't know, Annie hesitated, I guess Chandler's attitude itself is ironic. Why? I probed. Well, she went on, because Chandler envies all the wrong things, all the immoral things, for want of a better expression, that Gallagher represents. And there's irony in that.

Without another word, I picked up a piece of chalk and wrote a Joyce quotation on the board: My intention was to write a chapter of the moral history of my country and I chose Dublin for the scene because that city seemed to me the center of paralysis.

So, I said with my back still to them, where in all this beautiful Joycean mess is the epiphany?

The following week, they read two Hemingway stories: "The Killers" and "A Clean, Well-Lighted Place." I talked about Hemingway's style, so sparse, so direct, so poetic. I talked about Nick Adams. I talked about the three waiters, who become two, who become one, who become nothing. I had them write a brief essay on the points of reference in the two titles: What have they killed? And whom? Is there really a clean, well-lighted place, or is it a metaphor for something else? And as they wrote, I watched them, pretending to read the newspaper. Juan Kalel didn't show up that day, but I didn't give it much thought.

Annie Castillo and I had arranged to have a midmorning coffee in the faculty lounge. When she approached, I was smoking a cigarette and goading a neoliberal economics professor with Marxist gibes. Excuse me, I said, but this young lady has come to see me, and he immediately stood up and left.

Annie sat down. I asked her if she'd cut her hair. A little, she said, fiddling with her bangs. Should we get some coffee? I asked. All right, she said, and we walked together to the coffee machine. I saw that not only had she changed her hair but she was also wearing more makeup than usual. And she had on a tiny turquoise blouse that revealed her belly button and boldly accentuated her breasts and shoulders. Sugar? Please, she replied, and lots of cream.

Once we'd sat back down, we chatted about her other classes and, of course, the predictable uncertainty about her professional future. Her way of staring directly into my eyes made me so self-conscious that, from time to time, I was the one who had to glance down into my coffee or look for another cigarette or a piece of paper. She said she'd been thinking about the Joyce story. She said that a lot of the things he was pointing out about Dubliners, she found to be true of Guatemalans too. She said she'd never really liked literature, but that my class wasn't bad. Well, thank you, I said, and then asked her why she identified so strongly with Maupassant's narrator. I'm not sure, she replied after pausing to concentrate, as if trying to recall a memorized answer. I surround myself with people in order not to feel alone, Eduardo. But whether they're there or not, I always feel alone. Like the protagonist, I suppose. It's almost unbearable, you know? And she didn't say any more. And I decided not to ask any more.

Seeing the time, she said she was late. Algebra, she confided almost frantically. We both stood and I asked if she knew why Juan Kalel hadn't come to our last class. Who's Juan Kalel? she asked, and I just smiled. Annie stood there quietly but nervously, books clutched to her chest, eyes darting around. I asked her if she was all right. Of course, she replied. Why do you ask? I said nothing, toying with my cigarette, and she opened her mouth slightly, as though she were about to say something important or at least revealing, and then didn't.

Who can tell me what an "artificial nigger" is? I asked, in reference to the Flannery O'Connor story they'd read. Juan Kalel's seat was vacant again. A very tall girl's cell phone rang and, without my having to say anything, she picked up her things and left. What does the term "artificial nigger" actually refer to? I repeated, slightly irked. I was just about to explain that this was what those black lawn jockeys used to be called, and that they were very common in the South, and an unequivocal symbol of racism and slavery, when from the back row came perhaps the most or least literary response any of them could have given me. A kid with a shaved head called out: It refers to Michael Jackson.

After class, I went to the economics department and asked the secretary if something had happened to Juan Kalel, because he hadn't been to class in two weeks. She frowned and said she didn't know who Juan Kalel was. I nearly shouted that he was not only a first-year scholarship student but also a true poet. Juan Kalel has left the university, I heard the dean say from his office. Tell Eduardo to come in.

I was about to call you, he said as he shuffled some papers. Please, take a seat. He answered a phone call while responding to an e-mail, and told the secretary to give us a few minutes, that they'd talk a little later. How's your course going? he asked, signing something. I said fine. I was about to call you, Eduardo, he repeated. I'm afraid Juan Kalel has left the university. I asked if he knew why. Personal problems, I believe, he said, and it was obvious that he was going to give no more away. We were both silent, and I thought, stupidly, of some sort of tribute or homage to a fallen soldier. We got this a few days ago, he said, handing me an envelope. It came in the mail and I gave it to my secretary to pass on to you, but I imagine she simply hasn't had the time. The envelope was a grubby white. There was no return address, though the purple postmark was, of course, from Tecpán. I slipped it into my inside jacket pocket and stood up, thanking him. A real shame, the dean said, and I agreed, yes, a real shame.

Saturday, I climbed into my car at 7:00 A.M. and set off for Tecpán. I had Juan Kalel's letter and his notebook of poems with me, and nothing more. I'd sent him an e-mail to let him know I was coming, but it bounced back immediately. At the university, they'd refused to give me his actual address or his phone number, claiming that, officially, he was no longer a student and therefore his information had been, officially, deleted from the files. It was as though, officially, Juan Kalel had never existed.

On the way, I decided to stop for breakfast at my brother's house. He lived in San Lucas Sacatepéquez, some twenty kilometers from the capital, in a small village with the poetic-sounding name of El Choacorral.

I rang the bell for so long that he finally woke up. What are you doing here? he asked, propped in the doorway, still half-asleep. I told him I'd brought sweet rolls and champurradas and that I was on my way to Tecpán. He looked confused or maybe annoyed, and stepped aside to let me in. Still in robe and slippers, he showed me a few sculptures he was working on, in white marble, and then a plaster-cast mural he was planning to exhibit. Are you going to paint it? I asked, and he said yeah, maybe. I'm not really sure yet. He made a pot of coffee and we sat down to have breakfast on his terrace. It was cold, but mountain cold, which is different from a leaden, city cold. More chaste. More radiant. The air smelled clean, naked. I felt warmth on my face and saw that the sun was just beginning to peek out timidly from behind a green crag. I said I was on my way to Tecpán to try and find a student. Well, ex-student. Why's that? he asked, refilling my coffee. He dropped out. First year? Yeah, I said, and I was going to add that he was an economics major who wrote poetry, but then I thought better of it. Why did he drop out? I said I didn't know but that this was exactly what I wanted to find out. I'm guessing he's not just any student, he observed discreetly. No, I said, he's not. And we finished our coffee in silence.

Guatemalan place names never cease to amaze me. They can be like gentle waterfalls, or beautiful cats purring erotically, or itinerant jokes—it all depends. Back on the road, I drove through Sumpango, and every time I drive through Sumpango I feel obliged to read aloud the sign that says Sumpango, I don't know why. I went through El Tejar, which means place of roof tiles (where, unsurprisingly, they make a lot of roof tiles), and through Chimaltenango and then through Patzicía, which I also feel obliged to say aloud. All of these names are like charms; they cast some sort of linguistic spell, I thought as I drove, and I recited them like little prayers. Perhaps my favorites are the tenangos: Chichicastenango, Quetzaltenango, Momostenango, and Huehuetenango. I love them as words, as pure language. Tenango, I've been told, means place in Cakchikel, or maybe Kekchí. Then there's Totonicapán, whose heavy rhythm makes me think of an old warship, and Sacatepéquez, which sounds like the Spanish for take out your little thing, and makes me think of a woman masturbating. And I love Nebaj and Chisec and Xuctzul, so clipped and so raw, almost violent, though I've never been to any of them and would be hard-pressed even to find them on a map. But there are also towns with rustic, common names, names that have been put into a prosaic Spanish so they mean something to those who don't speak indigenous languages: Bobos is fools, Ojo de Agua means eye of water, and Pata Renca is lame foot. And in what's now a dangerous, war-torn area is Sal Si Puedes, get out if you can. But in my opinion, the Guatemalan town with the most characteristic and most (or perhaps least) creative name has got to be El Estor, located on the edge of Izabal Lake, where a couple of centuries ago a foreign family owned land and ranches and a famous store that all the locals called El Store, imitating the English. But of course they pronounced it El Estor, hence its current name. I suppose Guatemalan place names are the same as Guatemalans, when it comes down to it: a mix of delicate indigenous breezes and coarse Spanish phrases used by equally coarse conquistadors whose draconian imperialism is imposed in a ludicrous, brutal way.

When I reached Tecpán it was almost noon. I parked the car and walked into a place called Tienda Lucky. A plump woman was patting tortillas onto an enormous comal, but they were purple, or maybe deep blue. She must have noticed the look on my face because immediately she whispered that they were called black tortillas. Ah, I said, and took a seat.

A ranchera song could be heard in the distance. On the walls were three framed photos: what looked to be a Swiss cottage, a couple of white horses on a lawn, and a blond cop standing beside his shiny cruiser, complete with German shepherd at his side and a huge caption that read BEVERLY HILLS POLICE DEPARTMENT.

Out of nowhere, there appeared a girl who looked about ten, had beautiful features, and was decked out from head to toe in traditional clothing. She said hello. I ordered a beer and was about to light a cigarette when she tsked and pointed to a sign that said no smoking. But I can ask my aunt, she said in heavily accented Spanish, as though each word took a huge effort to pronounce. No, no, that's fine, and I put my cigarettes away.

At another table, a man in a hat and boots was drinking a bottle of India Quiché cola. He wore a piece of black cloth, a sort of apron-looking thing, hanging from his belt. He waved at me, but without looking.

The girl returned with my beer. I asked her name. Norma Tol, she said, smiling. That's pretty. How do you spell Tol? Tee, oh, el, she responded, drawing each letter in the air with her index finger. Tell me, Norma, is your aunt here? Yes, she said, and she didn't say any more. Could you call her over for me? I asked, and she ran to a door leading to the back. To the kitchen, I supposed. A bus overflowing with people crossed the road, leaving a thick trail of dust and noise in its wake. Good morning, said a very short woman dressed in black, and I saw that Norma was directly behind her, barricaded, protected. I said pleased to meet you, and apologized for troubling her. It's no trouble, she said in an accent even thicker than her niece's. Her hands were covered in some type of red sauce and she wiped them repeatedly on her skirt, rubbing hard. You must be Doña Lucky, I guess. That's right, muchacho, how can I help you? I explained that I was from the capital and that I was in Tecpán looking for a student. I'm his professor, well, I was his professor. Ah, she said, frowning, I see. And your student lives here? Yes, in Tecpán. And what's his name? His last name is Kalel. Juan Kalel is his name. She thought for a moment and then told me that there were a lot of Kalels in Tecpán, that it was a very common last name. I know his father is in charge of an orchard in Pamanzana, I continued, but she shook her head. And his mother works in a textile factory. Doña Lucky turned to the man in the hat and boots and asked him something in Cakchikel. I was going to say that Juan had a big scar on his right cheek, but I decided not to. Go to Pamanzana, the man told me. Yes, you go there, muchacho, Doña Lucky echoed. It is close and I think they will know him there. And then with some difficulty the two of them gave me directions.

I put a few bills on the table and stood. You don't want something to eat, muchacho? Doña Lucky asked, and I said thank you, no. Some pork rinds or a little estofado, maybe? No, thank you. You know estofado is the local dish in Tecpán? I said no, I didn't know. How do you prepare it, señora? Four different meats, she replied, pig, chicken, cow, and goat. You cook it in a big pot until the meat falls apart, with some thyme and laurel and orange juice and vinegar and a splash of beer and a splash of Pepsi. She smiled, but I couldn't tell if she was joking or not. Excuse me, I said to the man, who was still sitting there, what's the name of that cloth you have hanging from your belt? This? he asked, holding it up. It's a knee cloth, he said. Very traditional, he said. The kids don't want to wear them anymore, he said. I asked him what the Cakchikel name was, and cradling it like a wounded dove, he replied xerka. Excuse me? Xerka, he repeated, barely parting his lips. With an X? I asked, and he shrugged and said that he wouldn't know.

Technically, Pamanzana is a hamlet, though that's a pretty benevolent way to put it. Half a dozen adobe and rusted sheet-metal shacks lined the road, looking like they were about to collapse. I parked my car and walked to the tiny shop with a Rubios Mentolados cigarette sign over its door. Outside, a dog napped contentedly in the only spot of shade. Inside, a girl sat behind a metal grille, looking incarcerated, and she stood when she saw me. Good afternoon, I said. She just smiled uneasily. There was a strong smell of dried sardines, and instinctively I took a step back. I'm looking for the Kalel family, I said, for a young man named Juan Kalel, but the girl just smiled, more fearfully than pityingly. Do you know Juan Kalel? Crossing her arms, she murmured something unintelligible. His father tends an orchard here in Pamanzana. No response. I stood silently for a few seconds. I thought about all the bars that stood between us, about all those barriers, and I felt helpless. I bought a pack of cigarettes and, after lighting one, went back out to the street.

I walked toward the shacks, but there was no one in sight. The dog had awakened and was barking at something. A snake, maybe. Or a rat. I leaned against the car and for some reason thought of Annie Castillo, of her eyes, which had once struck me as molasses-colored, of her pallor, of her loneliness, and for a moment I felt a mixture of love and disdain and apprehension. I thought of all the students like Annie Castillo, who lived so close to hamlets like Pamanzana, but who also lived so blindly distant from hamlets like Pamanzana. And staring at the shacks and the dust, I thought about all the stories that, shut away in a more perfect world, we read and analyzed and discussed, as if reading them and analyzing them and discussing them actually mattered. And then I didn't want to think anymore.

I lit another cigarette. I was about to start reading some of Juan Kalel's poems, when I heard footsteps behind me. It was a woman dressed in black, carrying a big bag of fruit or vegetables. She wore a fine white mantilla on her head. She stopped just beside me, solemn and sweltering. You must be Señor Halfon, she said with no expression whatsoever, pronouncing my name the same way Juan Kalel did. I smiled, perplexed. She still looked somber. Her face was cheerless and weather-beaten, like an old sailor's. Juan has a book of yours, she said, and I recognized you from the photo. Are you his mother? She nodded just like her son. I told her I was very glad to meet her, that I'd come from the capital to speak to Juan a little but that I didn't know where to find him. Without looking at me, she said I was lucky, that she had only come to Pamanzana to get some cauliflower from the orchard her husband tended and that she was on her way back to Tecpán now. I offered her a ride and she accepted without a word.

Sitting uncomfortably in my car, she asked me if I was there to convince Juan to go back to school. Not at all, I said, I just want to speak to him. I decided not to mention his poetry. She was quiet for some time, staring out the window, holding her bag of cauliflower. I can assure you he won't be going back, she said suddenly. I was about to repeat that this wasn't why I'd come, but instead I said nothing. We need our Juan close by at the moment, she said, faltering. I didn't turn to look, but from the tone of her voice I could have sworn she was crying.

The Kalel house was on the outskirts of Tecpán, on the road to the Mayan ruins of Iximché. Once, as a kid, I visited Iximché with the family of a school friend, and the only memory I have is of eating green mango with lime and ground pumpkin seeds, and then vomiting it all up by the stones of some temple or altar. I remember my friend's mother fanning me with something as she gave me bitter sips of tonic water.

A black doll hung disconcertingly on the front door. Please, sit. Juan will be back very soon, his mother told me. The house looked clean and comfortable, in spite of everything. In one open area were the kitchen, a small table-cum-dining room, and a rustic black leatherette sofa. Candles cast a hazy light in one corner. I went over to look at a shelf with framed photos of the children at their First Communion, not realizing I'd been toying with a cigarette until Juan's mother brought in an ashtray. You can smoke, she said, placing it on the table. I thanked her and sat down, but I decided to slip it back into the pack. Without asking, she brought me a cup of plantain atol and then sat down beside me. I'd never tried plantain atol before. I asked her how it was made. She didn't reply. Do you know, Señor Halfon, why Juan left his studies? I said that I did not, that at the university they wouldn't say anything other than for personal reasons. That's what we requested, she said, looking down, but in an exaggerated way, as if her eyes would bore through the floor and into the ground. She remained like that until the door opened abruptly and Juan appeared in the doorway, holding hands with a girl of perhaps six or seven. He wore a too-small white shirt, with a too-small black vest over it. The girl looked like a miniature version of her mother: dressed in black, with a white mantilla on her head. I turned and saw that in the corner, around the candles, were wilted flowers and a rosary and some old photographs, and all of a sudden everything made sense.

For lunch we had turkey—which we call chompipe and they called chunto—and sweetened crookneck squash.

Then, as we walked together to the central square, Juan told me that his father had been sick for many years, that he had had prostate cancer and eventually it spread all over. He said that his father had refused to go to the capital to have a doctor look at it, that he preferred to keep working. My father died in the field, he said, and that was all he said. There was nothing else to say, I suppose. But the image of his father dying in an orchard, on land he tended that was not his, stayed with me.

Juan treated me to a cup of coffee. The best in Tecpán, he boasted, paying a woman who had her little table set out right in the center of the square. She poured a squirt of coffee extract, a little hot water, and a little milk into two plastic cups. When she said something in Cakchikel, Juan just smiled. In silence, we walked toward an empty bench.

This is yours, I said, handing him the notebook and the poem he'd mailed me. I thought he'd try to refuse them, but he took them with no comment whatsoever. A barefoot woman passed by, selling cashews. I've read your books, Halfon, Juan said, looking over at a group of men shining shoes beside the fountain. And then for a time, neither of us said anything. I wanted to tell him that it made perfect sense to me why he'd dropped out, that he didn't have to explain it. I wanted to tell him how much I missed him in class. I wanted to tell him to keep writing poetry. But there was no need for that. Someone like Juan Kalel could never abandon poetry, even if he wanted to, mostly because poetry would never abandon him. It wasn't a question of form, or aesthetics, but of something much more absolute, something much more perfect that had little or nothing to do with perfection.

A girl came up and said hello to Juan and the two of them began speaking in Cakchikel. It sounded beautiful, like drops of rain falling on a lake, perhaps. When she left, I asked Juan if he also wrote poems in Cakchikel. He said of course. I asked how he decided whether to write them in Spanish or Cakchikel. He was quiet for a time, looking out at the fountain where the shoe-shine boys gathered. I don't know, he said finally. I've never thought about it before. Then we fell back into that natural silence we had, as if neither of us really needed to say anything or as if everything between us had already been said, either way. The air smelled of roasted corn on the cob. In the distance, a boy was selling baby chicks, and people were ignoring a preacher. Do you know, Halfon, how to say poetry in Cakchikel? Juan asked suddenly. And I said no, I had no idea. Pach'un tzij, he said. Pach'un tzij, I repeated. And I savored the word for a time, taking pleasure in it purely for its sound, for the delectable lure of its pronunciation. Pach'un tzij, I said once more. Do you know what it means? he asked, and although I hesitated, I said no, but that it didn't really matter. Braid of words, he said. It's a neologism that means braid of words, he said. Pach'un tzij, he intoned, giving it an elegance that could only be gained through unskeptical spirituality. It's something like an embroidered blouse of words, like a huipil of words, he said, and that was all.

It had gotten late. The sun was starting to go down and we decided to walk back to Juan's house. Near the colonial church, an old man stood before a small white cage. We approached. He had a yellow canary in it and was whispering or singing softly to it. Juan told me that the canary was a fortune-teller, and I smiled. No, really, he said. How much?

I asked the old man. He raised two fingers. I took two coins from my pocket and handed them to him. But it's for him, I said, pointing to Juan: I'd rather know his future than mine. The old man took a wheel full of colored slips of paper and then whistled softly to the canary, placing the wheel in front of the bird. With its beak, the bird pecked out a pink slip of paper. Then the old man took it, whispered something to the bird, folded the paper in half, and handed it to Juan, who was staring fixedly at the canary. There was no tenderness in his stare, no compassion. Instead, he looked angry, almost violent, almost furious, as if the canary were divulging some dark secret. Juan unfolded the pink paper and read it in silence. I simply watched, also silent, and maybe it was the streetlight, or maybe it was something else, but I could see the purple scar clearly on his right cheek, which now looked like much more than a blow from a machete. And then very slowly, as if emerging from a nightmare, Juan began to smile. I thought of asking him what the paper said, asking him what future the canary had predicted for him, but I decided against it. Some smiles are not meant to be understood. Juan said something to the old man in Cakchikel, slipped the pink paper into his shirt pocket, and looking up at the sky said it would be getting dark soon.

Twaining

I arrived in Durham wanting to vomit. The passenger next to me, a huge black guy with the friendliest southern accent possible, had been talking to me throughout the three-hour flight about the furniture business in North Carolina, while the plane heaved and shook like a damn spinning top. Try sucking on an ice cube, he suggested when he saw me turning pale, or green, or both. That always helps. I closed my eyes for the last stretch of the journey, and when we finally landed and I dared to open them again, the big black guy was fanning me worriedly with one of the in-flight magazines. Nice people, southerners.

I'd studied engineering in the same area, just twenty minutes from Durham, but I hadn't been back for twelve years. Why would I? That prim nostalgia that Americans drum up for their alma mater has always seemed really pathetic to me. I walked out of the airport and the November chill made me feel better, or at least not so dizzy. I wandered between taxis and suitcases. Because of the tinted glass, it took me a while to make out my last name in the window of a plush limousine—well, not exactly a limousine, but a Cadillac or a Lincoln, which as far as I was concerned came to pretty much the same thing. I asked the driver if I had time to smoke a cigarette and he said of course, that we were still waiting for a passenger from Utah. I sat down on a bench. He stayed on his feet. I offered him a Camel, but he looked serious and shook his head. We talked about the weather, though it's possible that I'm wrong and that's just how I remember it. He was surprised to learn that I came from Guatemala and more surprised when I told him I'd been born there and still lived there. But your English is excellent, he remarked, and I said thanks very much, yours too. He just exhaled an enormous cloud of cold air.

After a while the passenger from Utah appeared. Harold Lewis. Professor of political science at Brigham Young University. A Mormon, of course. He was in Durham to take part in a conference on Mark Twain. Me too, I told him, and he was obviously surprised to see me in jeans, unshaven, and smoking like some Latino revolutionary. Yes, I told him, I was a university professor as well, but I don't think he believed me or perhaps he did and just decided to look proud and disdainful. There was something shepherdlike about Lewis, though I'm not even sure what I mean by that. We put our suitcases in the trunk of the limousine, I took a last drag on my cigarette and jumped into the backseat of the sumptuous vehicle with the excitement of a child arriving at an amusement park. The driver told us that we could relax, that we were fifteen minutes from the hotel. Lewis asked me where I was from, and when I told him he raised his eyebrows, but I don't know why. Gringos. I turned to look out at the immense pine forests that girded the highway, and I remembered what a three- or four-year-old girl once asked when she saw the trees passing by her car window (Why are the trees running backward?), and smiled. Some memories are harmless. Or at least they seem harmless. Look, how tragic, Lewis said, pointing to a dead deer on the road. Real common, said the driver, to see deer run over around these parts. It occurred to me then, as a limousine carrying a Guatemalan and a Mormon rumbled past deer carcasses toward an academic conference on Mark Twain, that I was in the wrong place. Sometimes, just briefly, I forget who I am.

We arrived at the Duke Inn. Out of habit, I gave a few dollars to the driver and found it odd that Lewis didn't do the same, but I didn't overthink it either. There were dozens of golfers in the lobby. The click of their spikes on the parquet floor, not to mention the cocktails golfers seem to need after a round of eighteen holes, made me think of my father. Besides being a hotel and conference center, the Duke Inn was also a private golf club. The receptionist, an Indian or Pakistani girl I thought was quite cute, handed me my room key and a folder with instructions and time-tables for the days ahead, and I saw with relief that I still had an hour before the welcome dinner. I asked the girl if I could smoke in my room. Looking at her computer screen, she told me no, that she was very sorry but she didn't have any more smoking rooms. Oh wait a minute, she said with unnecessary excitement, there is one, but I'm afraid it's for disabled people. That's no problem, I'm a writer, I wanted to say, but instead I said nothing and she explained to me that the room was designed for guests in wheelchairs. That won't bother me, I told her. Excuse me a moment, she said, and conferred in whispers with a somewhat effeminate man. Her boss, I assumed. No problem, Mr. Halfon, I just need you to sign here, next to the X, and I signed right away, without even reading the damn thing.

Like some Gulliver, like Alice in an exotic wonderland, or even better, like Snow White in the cottage of the Seven Dwarfs—that's how I felt. Everything was lower down than usual. The bed, the desk, the TV, the nightstand, the sink, the toilet, even the peephole you looked through to see who was at the door was at waist level. There were rails everywhere and a ramp in the shower. I'm in an invisible circus, I thought, and lit a cigarette. I liked feeling submerged in a more literary environment, or who knows, maybe I just liked feeling bigger.

I took a shower. Wrapped in a towel, I decided to lie down for a minute before going back downstairs, and I dozed without meaning to. I may have dreamed that I was Mark Twain or someone very similar to Mark Twain, sailing down the Mississippi River while writing that I was sailing down the Mississippi River. It was already late when I woke up, but I got ready quickly and arrived in the dining room on the first floor just as they were serving the salads. A young woman greeted me with her eyes and came up to me. Mr. Halfon, I assume. I apologized. Your seat is at that table over there, and she pointed to it. There were sixteen people invited to the conference and, as I would realize later, I was the only foreigner. I introduced myself as I sat down. A young woman named Mary Catherine something—I can't remember her last name—told me that she taught economics at Yeshiva University in New York. Disconcerted, I asked her if she was Jewish. God no, she said, and I didn't want to inquire further. A shy young man was working on his doctoral thesis on English poets of the fourteenth or fifteenth century—I can't remember which and I can't remember his name. I'm a professor of public choice at Notre Dame, an older woman told me, and I still have no idea what public choice is, despite her having spent more than twenty minutes explaining it to me. To my right, a little old man was taking sips of his zucchini soup in silence. He must be at least ninety, I thought as I watched his hand tremble every time he tried to bring it to his mouth. Hi, I said to him. He put his spoon on the table and glanced up. He looked at me for a while, as though trying to decide whether or not it was worth talking to me. He had bright blue eyes, long fingernails, and a scraggy beard that somehow seemed fake. Did you know that zucchinis are an aphrodisiac? he whispered. Really? I asked. No, he said, but that's what I tell my wife so she'll make them a lot. He smiled. But please, kid, he said conspiratorially, patting my forearm, don't tell her that. He smiled again. I can't be sure, but I think I grew fond of Joe Krupp straight away, even before I knew who he was or what he did.

After dinner and some pretty dull speeches, they herded us all into another room to drink a few cocktails. Hospitality hour, they called it. I drank a port and, without saying a word to anyone, decided to slip back to my Lilliputian room. I don't like drinking with intellectuals. When I got there, I saw that there were two little chocolates on the pillow and that the TV was tuned to a channel offering porn films for seven dollars each. I was told once that the average man watches three minutes of a porn film and I wondered whether it was different for women. I still don't know the answer. I ate both chocolates. I went out onto the little balcony to read a bit about Twain's life and smoke a cigarette, but I hadn't even opened the book when my eyelids started to droop. As I stubbed my cigarette out, I thought I could hear sobs coming from the balcony to my right, and peering over cautiously, I managed to see the dark trembling silhouette of a woman sitting with her arms folded. She was whimpering softly, like a baby tired of crying. I suppose she also saw me but it was very dark, so I couldn't be sure. I thought of asking her if she was all right, if she needed anything. Then I thought it would be inappropriate and just went silently back into my room and fell asleep.

I had a cheese omelette for breakfast with a few cups of coffee—really terrible coffee—and managed to squeeze in a last cigarette, freezing outside with the golfers and the other outcast smokers, before the talks started.

The first session of the conference was about the opening chapters of *Huckleberry Finn*, and on the whole the contributions weren't very interesting. That's what multidisciplinary conferences are like: they have little or no discipline. Each person wrestles the discussion toward their own discipline, including me. Feeling a bit bored, I told them it was years since I'd looked at Twain's work. Not since I was a kid. But I can no longer just think of him like that, I said, I mean, like a writer of adventure stories for children. Deep down, he's quixotic. Silence. Right from the first paragraph,

I went on, the book is absolutely quixotic or Cervantine. The narrator, in this case Huckleberry Finn, mentions a previous work called *The Adventures of Tom Sawyer*. And I read aloud: That book was made by Mr. Mark Twain, and he told the truth, mainly. That's a Cervantine trick, ladies and gentlemen, a self-referential mention of the author. Silence. Some pages later, I continued, while they looked for the page despite my not having said which one it was, Tom Sawyer tells the narrator, Huck Finn, that if he wasn't so ignorant and had read a book called *Don Quixote*, he'd know that everything is done by enchantment. Think about the fact that Twain himself quotes Cervantes, I said, and waited in vain for some kind of reaction. Now, why do I think this is so important? I paused like a good professor, until I could feel all fifteen pairs of eyes on me. The relationship between these two characters, between Tom Sawyer and Huck Finn, is very similar to the relationship between Sancho Panza and Don Quixote, a fact proved as the book continues, especially by Tom's treatment of his friend Huck, and by the ending, and by the attitude that Tom adopts after reading heroic tales. He's quixotted, I said, and took a sip of tepid water for the pure theatrics of it. Nothing. Silence. Whether it was because they'd never read *Don Quixote* or because such a heterogeneous group weren't interested in narrative or even because they hadn't understood a fucking thing I'd said, my point of view was of little interest to them. In the hours that followed, they continued to talk about slavery and politics and a load of other deeply sterile and not very literary ideas.

They served us pasta and vegetables for lunch. Next to me sat a history professor from a small university in Idaho, or Washington, or one of those other states on the Pacific coast, a man fat as a bear, whose only interest was practicing his awful Spanish. After the meal I needed a cigarette. I tried to get up but felt a hand on my shoulder, and heard a slow, hoarse voice asking me where I was going. It was Joe Krupp. I then realized he'd been the only one not to speak at all during the morning session. You in a hurry, kid? he asked. I said I wasn't, that I was just going to smoke a cigarette. He stood there without speaking, looking through the huge windowpane out into the void. Ah, you smoke, he remarked. I said nothing. But quitting smoking is the easiest thing in the world, my friend. And then he added, very seriously: I've done it thousands of times. His hand was still on my shoulder. I like walking after I eat. What do you say we walk for a while, kid? he said, indicating the golf course with his sky blue eyes.

The path curled over the man-made prairie. Every now and then we had to stand to one side, to make way for a few golfers dressed up like clowns and chasing white balls in their charming little mechanized carts. Joe Krupp walked like he spoke: slowly, serenely, as though his feet and his words were in no hurry to get where they were going, or as though they weren't going anywhere at all. How wonderful life would be if we were born in old age, I thought as I listened to him talk of his childhood in Missouri, of his experiences in the war, of how he had met his wife. Kruppowsky. Polish, originally. I thought of my grandfather and the bottle of whiskey we'd drunk together while he told me about Sachsenhausen and Auschwitz and the Polish boxer. Do you like living in Guatemala, kid? he asked, and then allowed me to speak for a long time without interrupting, one hand behind his back and the other resting on my shoulder. I don't know whether this was to steady himself or out of affection. Both, I'd like to think. I lit another cigarette and we walked for a while in silence until he told me that he'd found the comparison between Tom Sawyer and Don Quixote interesting. Very interesting, kid, but you should know that in Thomas A. Tenney's book, *Mark Twain: A Reference Guide*, there are more than ten essays on the relationship between Miguel de Cervantes and Mark Twain, one of them in Spanish, if I remember rightly. I kept quiet. And I should tell you, he continued after another quartet of golfers had passed, that that book only lists works published up to 1975, and I'm sure there are other papers you could look up that have been written since then. We sat down on a bench next to an enormous cypress tree. For some reason I'd assumed Joe Krupp was an economist or perhaps a historian, and I told him this, a little ashamed. No, far from it, he said, laughing, I was a professor of literature for nearly fifty years, kid, here at Duke University most of the time, and I've been studying Mr. Twain for nearly as long. (I'd learn later, browsing in the library, that Joe Krupp was one of the most important academics specializing in Twain's work.) I stuttered that I was sorry, that I didn't know. And I bet you also didn't know that Mr. Twain spent some time in Central America. What do you think of that? he said, and let out a sharp laugh. That's right kid, in Nicaragua, around the corner from your own country, in 1866. I hadn't known that either. Mr. Twain, he called him, with that almost sacred respect you can only develop over long years of literary veneration, and it occurred to me that, in a quite unusual way, Joe Krupp spoke like Mark Twain himself must have spoken. Suddenly a cat came up to us, rubbed up against my legs and then, when I bent down to stroke it, ran away. I noticed the old man give a strange smile. Like a man in love, I thought, and then corrected myself: like a man in sadness. Mr. Twain wrote that one of the most notable differences between a cat and a lie, he said, is that a cat only has nine lives. He smiled and got up with a little difficulty. So, my friend, you can never believe what Mr. Twain says about anything, even his own name. We walked back in silence, his hand on my shoulder. I remember him telling me in all seriousness that he was tired and needed to rest for a while so he could go out dancing later with his wife. Tangos, he said.

There was another session that afternoon. I didn't say much. I drank cup after cup of an almost transparent coffee in order not to fall asleep during the tedious intellectual debate on conscience and morality in Twain's characters. They focused on Jim and Huck. Joe Krupp remained silent again, listening and appraising with an enigmatic look that seemed to me like the mixture of pity and mockery that you see on the face of a mime. When we'd finished, they took us all by minibus to a Greek restaurant. I ate roast lamb and drank enough wine to endure the moronic conversation about terrorism and the war in Iraq that, according to everyone there, the United States was winning. Idiots, I whispered, already half-drunk. I was tired when I got back but didn't feel like sleeping. Stretched out on my bed and looking at the images on the muted television without really seeing them, I smoked for a while in silence. I went out onto the balcony, hoping to see the woman next door crying. There was nobody there. I looked for my coat.

The lobby was all but deserted. I went into the bar and asked the waiter if they sold cigarettes. There's a machine over there, sir, he replied and he took me over to show me. Nice people, southerners. I was just about to ask for a beer at the bar when I heard my name. It was Harold Lewis, the Mormon, sitting alone in a corner, and I suppose he saw the confusion on my face because he raised his glass straight away. Don't worry, it's apple juice. He explained that sometimes he found it very difficult to sleep, especially in hotels, and told me to join him for a while. I mumbled some poor excuse about being tired or having reading to do or whatever it was. And see you tomorrow.

I needed a bit of fresh air and went out to the golf course. I walked a few holes, smoking, shivering from the cold but happy to be outside. The full moon cast a gray light on everything. It was a bland, tasteless gray that for some reason reminded me of old neorealist Italian films. A little way off, a strange shape caught my eye. I thought some golfer must have left his bag of clubs on the grass, but when I got closer I realized that the large mass was moving, just slightly. A deer, I thought, and carried on walking toward it. I was perhaps ten or fifteen yards away when I heard a squeal and ran to hide behind the nearest tree. She had her shirt open. She was on top of him, thrusting rhythmically and moaning as if she were alone in the universe. Without being able to make out what he was saying, I could hear him whispering, his voice getting louder while his hands grabbed desperately at her stomach and breasts. I stayed where I was, in spite of the cold, watching them copulate on the fairway like two wild animals, until after a while I decided to withdraw in silence. I don't know why. Maybe out of embarrassment, or maybe because I'm an average man and my three minutes were up. Who knows.

I didn't sleep much. For breakfast, I had a roll with cream cheese, and arrived late and dozy to the last session.

I poured myself a coffee while everyone discussed *Life on the Mississippi*, a fairly fragmented, semiautobiographical work, which recounts the vicissitudes of Twain's life on the steamboats of the Mississippi. For nearly three hours they debated the author's economic ideas, his conception of identity, his criticism of the fake southern aristocracy, and his notion of liberty. At one inopportune moment, I pointed out that here again Twain mentioned his admiration for *Don Quixote*. What an idiot, I thought, and I'm sure everyone else thought the same. But while I talked about Tom and Huck and Sancho and that Sad-Faced Knight, I thought I sensed some kind of stylistic correlation between the two authors, or no, rather than stylistic it was philosophical, cosmological, but it vanished again just as quickly as I'd found it, and right in the middle of my argument, as though I'd simply run out of gas, I stopped talking.

Smiling strangely again, for the first time in two days Joe Krupp asked to speak, said that humor is everything, that humor is our salvation, that humor is mankind's greatest blessing—which sounded to me like a quote, but I didn't want to interrupt him—and then, with his languid Mark Twain voice, he started telling jokes. All kinds of jokes. For nearly half an hour. I think I might have been the only

person who understood straight away where he was heading, or maybe I didn't understand at all.

And as we're in a golf club, said Joe Krupp to the group
of confused intellectuals, well, that's where I'll finish. All
right. One day a man walks into the women's bathroom at
a private golf club, accidentally, of course, and when he gets
out of the shower he realizes that all his clothes are gone.
Quite a fix, Joe Krupp said slowly, as though he himself
were trying to remember or invent the punch line. Then,
he continued after a pause, the man hears some women's
voices and puts a towel round his head to hide his face, but
remaining otherwise completely naked. I could have sworn
that while he was talking, the sky blue gaze of the old man
settled on me, as though there were no one else in that huge
cold conference room. And so when the man tries to run
out of the bathroom, he bumps into the three women, who
are shocked at first but then start looking him over closely,
examining him, as it were. Joe Krupp laughed a devilish
little laugh, with that mischievousness that only old age
can absolve. That man isn't my husband, says the first. That
man isn't my husband either, says the second. That man,
says the third, isn't even a member of this club.

Epistrophy

The first time I heard Milan Rakić play was a few years ago in the ruins of San José el Viejo. A pigeon had landed in its nest way up in the vaulted roof, directly above the Serbian pianist, who played on as though the rejoicing of the hungry chicks and the courageous flapping of the pigeon's wings were notes that had been set down in the score by Rachmaninoff himself.

I'd arrived in Antigua a little late, and there was Lía, waiting for me in the Café del Conde, ripping the cellophane off of a pack of cigarettes with her teeth, and an ice-cold beer on the table. As if afraid to sit down, I stood there explaining that a truckload of chickens had overturned on the highway, holding up traffic in both directions for hours, and she just kept looking at me with as much incredulity as she could muster, which was a lot. Well, we've missed the talk on neo-baroque Italian architecture, she said in a silky voice, looking at her watch. I know. And the Irish children's choir, she added. I thought about telling her I wasn't in the mood to listen to some pretentious guy talk about neo-baroque Italian architecture, or to witness the alleluias of a chorus of pale Irish kids, or to watch the spasmodic

51

strutting of some Far Eastern dance company, or to sub-
mit myself to the cheap melodramas of Salvadorean theater,
or to partake—begging the pardon of any hooligans in the
stands—in any of the activities at the biannual festival of
culture in Antigua, Guatemala. I just let out a sigh. Oh
well, Lía said suddenly, maybe it's for the best. And she half
smiled. Come on, give me a kiss, she said, yanking down on
my shirt. Her mouth tasted like a desert island.

It was dark already and we drank our beer in silence.
There was a strange stone fish next to us, spitting water
vertically, halfheartedly, as if gargling. Every now and then
Lía would lift up her hand so I could take a drag on her
cigarette. Oxygen administered by the loveliest of nurses.
She said she'd already checked us into our room. The same
one? I asked, and she smiled uneasily. The same one, Dudú.
She'd been calling me Dudú ever since she'd spent some
time in Salvador de Bahía, doing Capoeira, sunbathing
naked or half-naked, and of course learning Portuguese.
She came back with a nickname for me like I was some
midfielder on the Brazilian soccer team, as well as with her
pubis shaved smooth. It seems impossible to me, incon-
ceivable even, to resist falling in love with someone whose
name was Lía and who had come back from vacation with
her pubis shaved smooth.

Over another beer, we talked about the decadence of
youth, about counts who walled up their adversaries, about
superstring theory (Lía might have been studying medicine,
but she had a thing for quantum physics), about oral sex
according to Tibetan Tantra and oral sex according to a Cor-
tázar story. Seeing the time, she said there was a marimba
concert at Panza Verde. I kissed her neck. Come on, Dudú,

just for a bit, she said as she closed her eyes and lifted her chin slightly, offering me still more of her neck. I paid for the beers.

We walked over to Panza Verde, or Green Belly, a restaurant that flaunts that questionably noble nickname for the people of Antigua—for their growing as well as eating so many greens, I'd been told. The men were in jackets and ties, the women all dressed up in furs and jewels and magnificent evening gowns, almost all of them black (for our part, we were looking particularly swanky in leather sandals and old T-shirts). Someone, somewhere, was playing the marimba. Several ambassadors, with champagne and chortling potbellies, were chatting at the back. The members of an Austrian quartet, who Lía told me had been playing Mozart that morning, were sticking together around a table, fearful, I suppose, of getting separated and having to face alone the dangers of the Third World. The Venezuelan baritone could be heard bawling about politics and, like any good Venezuelan, clucking incessantly about Chávez. There were some Guatemalan poets, drunk already, telling jokes about queers and about Rigoberta Menchú. Charming, I whispered as we dodged perfumes and waved hello and made our way straight to the bar in search of two tequilas and a little privacy.

A dark-skinned girl asked us what kind of tequila. We've got all sorts, she concluded, smiling conspiratorially, as if to say comrades, we'll die here together. Ándele, cried Lía, white tequila, the best you've got. And we toasted the dark-skinned girl. Another? she said, wiping down the bar with a filthy cloth. Her hands looked too small to me. Then they looked like two muddy starfish. Then like two sad, puffed-up tarantulas locked in a territorial contest neither was ever going to win. And raising our glasses once more, we toasted Lee Marvin (we'd seen *The Killers* recently, the second film to be based on the story by Hemingway, shot in 1964 and directed by Don Siegel, during the entire filming of which Mr. Marvin was utterly, beatifically drunk). Someone left a tray of canapés in front of us.

Look, over there, said Lía, and I followed her gaze. A guy with long hair was drinking red wine at the far end of the bar. On his own. As if forgotten amid all the chaos. Hold this, she said, giving me the lit cigarette as she stood up. Lía was like that. She loved rescuing frail little birds and stray dogs. Once, when she was a girl, for her kindheartedness, she'd gotten a bite taken out of her left thigh by a huge, dirty English sheepdog.

May I introduce Milan Rakić? Pleased to meet you, he said in impeccable Spanish, albeit with an unabashedly Argentinian lilt. I asked if he was Argentinian. Serbian, he said, but my girlfriend's from Buenos Aires. Gde si bre čoveče, I declaimed. Hey, you know Serbian? he cried, giving me a slap on the back. Lía smiled. As if, I said—too many Kusturica films. Then I said I remembered having read something about a Serbian pianist in the festival program. Yours truly, he exclaimed, smiling and jerking his thumb at his chest. And have you already played? Lía asked. He lit a cigarette. Tomorrow, at midday, he said, sighing a nervous or possibly desperate lungful of smoke.

There was another stool there, but Milan remained standing between the two of us. I guessed he must have been about my age. He was wearing a light, loose-fitting tortilla-colored shirt and his fingers were heaped with heavy silver rings. His dark, straight hair almost covered his face entirely, and for some reason I started thinking about bridal veils, which Lía really had a thing about. Maybe because of the shape of his eyes, maybe because of something else much harder to pin down, he seemed to me to have a nocturnal look about him. The look of someone who can see properly only at night, or who wants to see properly only at night. The look of a vampire, but a sad, well-meaning vampire who doesn't need any more blood, just a long splash in holy water.

We ordered three tequilas. So you're from Belgrade? Lía asked him. Yes, Belgrade, though I've lived abroad for many years, he said, keeping his gaze fixed on the dark-skinned girl as she served the three drinks. Thanks so much, Miriam, he said flirtatiously. And where have you lived? I asked. What a beauty, he whispered, and then, as if exiting a dark, narrow tunnel, he said he'd studied music in Italy, in Russia, and currently in New York. A little confused, I sat looking at the dark-skinned girl with the Mayan features until Lía gave my leg a good hard pinch. And what will you play tomorrow, Milan? she asked. Who knows, it's always a mystery, he said mysteriously, with a hint of showy dogmatism. Then he said: Maybe a little Rachmaninoff, or Saint-Saëns, or Liszt, or Stravinsky. Ah, Charlie Parker's favorite, I said just to say something. Milan smiled. You like jazz? I told him that in my last or second-to-last incarnation, before making the small leap over into a Judeo-Latin American cosmology, I must have been a third-rate black jazz musician playing in some brothel in Kansas City or Storyville (a name so lovely, it seems made up), although I could just as easily have been a black hooker from

Kansas City or Storyville who spent all night fucking to the rhythm played by some third-rate jazz musician. Which is to say, I said with all the seriousness of a poor forgotten harlequin, I've got jazz deep in my gonads. And I downed the tequila. What kind of jazz do you like? Milan asked, and before I could reply, I felt Lía's warm hand over my mouth. This one I know by heart, she said. He likes pure jazz, she said. He likes anyone who plays with swing, right? Although Dudú has never managed to explain to me what swing is. I licked her fingers. Laughing, she wiped her hand on my thigh. You can't explain swing, Milan murmured. I like Bird and early Miles and Coltrane and Tatum and Powell and Mingus, I told him. But my true love is Monk. Ah! cried Milan after a little sip of his tequila, the magnificent Thelonious Monk. And then, as if we were invoking the names of Aztec warriors or of strange Nordic runes, we took turns reciting the titles of everything written by Melodious Thunk, as his wife called him, every single piece, in a jumble that somehow appeared organized by the stiff fingers of that eccentric pianist of dissonances and berets and mystic trances and the cheeks of a happy minnow. Lía listened patiently to us, dropping in questions here and there. You can easily recognize a Monk composition by its style, I replied, but it's not easy, even for true devotees, to know exactly which piece it is. He didn't go near the piano in his later years, Milan replied. I think epistrophy is a botanical term, I replied, and Milan immediately gave me a mocking smile. It doesn't mean anything, he said. That son of a bitch made it up. But isn't epistrophe also a rhetorical term, something repetitive, very musical, asked Lía, as in the famous: They're born to thieves, raised among thieves, they study to be thieves, and finally become thieves themselves? And though she was right—Milan responded to the Cervantes quotation with a sour expression that wouldn't make sense to me till the following day—neither of us answered her. I pointed out that, in an interview with George Simon in *Metronome*, Monk had said it was a botanical term, signifying the reversion of abnormal to normal. And you believe him, Eduardito? Utter nonsense, he said. I looked it up myself. There are people who say, in the same way, that Monk took the concept from Greek mythology, from epistrophe as associated with Aphrodite and love and sexuality and other such crap, but that's all nonsense too. Milan paused, and it struck me that he even spoke musically. He said: Some things signify nothing and are beautiful all the same. Epistrophy, he said, and the word fell like a dead dragonfly in a bowl of warm lentil soup. Then, in a fatherly gesture that could well have had more of a spiritual meaning among old Yugoslavs, or could equally have meant nothing at all, Milan, who still hadn't sat down, stroked my head fondly.

No one said anything for a few moments, a fitting silence, full of the most intense dignity. Lía stubbed out her cigarette, said excuse me, and went to the bathroom. Milan walked over to the bar and asked the dark-skinned girl for a glass of red wine. And stayed there, flirting with her. A theater director came over to say hello, but I acted uninterested and he soon went off again. Anything for you? said Milan, and I was struck once again by the very Argentinian way he spoke Spanish. A beer, please. He asked me about Lía and I told him her full name was Lía Gandini, that we'd met during the intermission of a performance of some comic

monologues after putting up with one very bad-tempered
Italian actor and another quite charming one, and that we'd
been introduced by a mutual friend, whom we went on to
ignore as we drank red wine for the rest of the intermission,
too dry (the wine) and too short (the intermission), and I
rambled on about one of Dario Fo's tigers that I liked and
she smiled at me with those endless eyelashes of hers. Milan
didn't appear to pick up on the reference. I like her long
neck, he said. Like a swan, he said. Like one of Modigliani's
women. I guess, I said, and took a sip of beer. I asked him
if there had been any difference between studying classical music in the States and in Europe. God, he said, huge.
And he sat down on Lía's stool. The thing is, he said, the
Americans like classical compositions to be played as if one
were a machine or a robot. Devoid of all emotion. As if
you weren't there. The music always exactly the same. What
they want, he said, is to eliminate the interpreter's personal-
ity altogether. He lit a cigarette and, smiling at the dark-
skinned girl, thought for a moment. Do you know who
Lazar Berman was? No idea. A great pianist, he told me. A
Liszt expert. A Russian Jew who fought against the music
of Chopin the Pole, he said, and immediately jumbling
up his words, I had thoughts of the Polish boxer fighting
every night, followed by thoughts of my grandfather fighting with Polish words. I studied under Berman as a child,
Milan said, in Italy. Want one? he asked, and I accepted a
cigarette. I remember that on the first day, in his studio, I
played Liszt's Sonata in B Minor, a very complex piece, and
the old Jew, sitting on his enormous red velvet sofa, didn't
say a word. Nothing. The second day, I went back to his studio, began playing the same piece and, straight off, Berman

got up and began tapping the window with his cane, like this, very softly. Milan, after a long sip of wine, dried his mouth on the sleeve of his shirt. The old man shouted at me in Russian: You're playing the piece the same way you did yesterday, child. I kept my mouth shut as Berman carried on tapping the window with his cane. I thought he'd lost it. But then he walked over to me, very slowly, put a hand on my shoulder and, with a devilish smile, whispered: Haven't you noticed, my boy, that it's raining today? A big difference, Milan said, moving aside so that Lía could sit down. Tomorrow, Eduardito, I'll play a little Liszt, he concluded, as if this confirmed the truth of his anecdote, and off he went to chat with the dark-skinned girl.

The restaurant seemed to be emptying out. Lía had a sip of my beer. I stroked her forearm, and she, pouting semierotically—reminding me of a very young Marilyn Monroe, or at least of a very young Natalie Portman doing a poor but sweet impression of Marilyn Monroe—said she wanted to go. Then, exaggerating the pout still further, she said she was itching to draw in her almond-colored notebook. I downed my beer in two gulps.

Standing up, I said to Milan we'd be coming to listen to him the next day. Definitely. He hugged us both at the same time. A three-way hug, my dears, he said with a fake, forced laugh, the laugh of someone who didn't really want to laugh.

Before we got to the room, Lía had already taken her bra off. She liked to take it off while we were driving in the car or walking along, because she knew I liked to imagine her suddenly braless. We began stopping every now and then in the middle of the street to kiss, and she'd take my hand and place it on her cold, bare breasts, shuddering as though no one had ever touched her there. It was hard to tell, tight in each other's arms, which one of us was trembling. Maybe neither. Then we'd carry on walking, impatient, a little giddy. The bra in her handbag or maybe forgotten on the ground or maybe dangling like some enormous black pod from the branch of a tree.

Then the uproar of beer and tequila sex. A naked thing that trembled with a thousand legs and a thousand hands and a thousand guava-flavored tongues that could never be enough to make love with. Not saying a word or at least not saying words that made any sense, which always mean more. We ended up half-asleep, connected, inseparable, never finishing (sex is always better in gerunds), until at daybreak I heard the far-off cry of a child or a rooster and felt a breeze across my chest and saw her warm and sitting up in bed. She glowed amber. The almond-colored note-book was open on her lap.

Lía used to draw her orgasms.

Since our first time, whenever we finished, she'd get up, make her way across the room completely naked, and come back to bed with a small almond-colored notebook. Then, leaning on one elbow or sitting or sometimes kneel-ing, she'd begin to sketch the orgasm or orgasms that she'd experienced and that were still fresh in her vaginal mem-ory; to make graphs of them for me, like a scientist would, with everything from convulsions to climaxes, spasms, changes in temperature, and liquid overflows. In general she'd sketch a line that would resemble a mountain or a series of mountains of different heights and widths. Sometimes the plateau was short; often it was round; sometimes it extended horizontally for what appeared to be several kilometers. From somewhere, almost always (but not always) out of a crater, fluvial jets would burst up. Bristling, zigzagging lines would spring out very sporadically on the slopes, like miniature lightning bolts, but I've no idea what they meant: that was her one secret, she used to say, and it was of the utmost importance. So, whenever one of these zigzags sprouted up, I'd feel ludicrously satisfied without knowing why. Other times, though, it wouldn't be mountains she'd draw, but clouds or cotton spirals or something of the kind: throbbing, dense, closed ellipses. She explained to me that she didn't know how else to represent it, that this was how she perceived her whole body: as a light, palpating mass. I envied her. Other times, the drawing would resemble a grapevine without any grapes. Other times: a knot of electric cables set on top of a post. Other times: a prickly fossil. Other times: the map of some African country, perhaps Angola or Namibia. Only once, on a night in that same room in Antigua, had Lía told me it couldn't be drawn, her head buried in my shoulder, possibly crying, trembling meekly, her warm vagina dampening my thigh as the last little drops of some ineffable pleasure drained away. And again I envied her or maybe I envied the whole female sex. But usually she'd carry out her studied scribbles with the dedication of a Flemish painter, revealing to me the details, the signs, the keys to interpret her most unfathomable mysteries.

With my eyes closed, I caressed her bare back and began to dream of an archipelago of freckles. I could hear the rustling sound of the pen as it glided over the paper, followed by a brief silence, and then the rustle of the pen again. I felt a kiss on my belly. Ready, Lía said, and curling up beside me, passed me the notebook.

A raging sea viewed from a small boat.

That was what the sketch looked like. I wanted to ask her what it meant, but I felt her rhythmic breathing on the back of my neck and almost immediately fell into a deep sleep as well.

I don't know if it was when I woke up or if I was still dreaming when I remembered that Liszt had been the lover of a princess who was related to Wittgenstein, and had also been Wagner's father-in-law. I told Lía this and she, emerging from the white sheets, lazy as a snake shedding her skin, said it was time for a shower.

We had coffee and champurradas in the hotel restaurant. Wet patches from Lía's chestnut-colored hair adorned her grayish T-shirt. She chatted away about her dreams (she always remembered them in great detail). Listening to her, it occurred to me that her husky, ethereal voice sounded as though she was talking to me completely submerged in a bathtub of milk.

The audience inside the ruins of San José el Viejo was murmuring bashfully. The air was cold, congealed, as if still for centuries, and an exquisite light spread harmoniously throughout the great vaulted space. Ranks of folding chairs had been set out facing a grand piano that rose up ahead of them, a solitary thing on its raised platform. I thought of a black ship about to set sail.

We took seats in the back row. Lía shushed warm kisses in my ear. A boy of three or four was kneeling on the seat in front and every so often he'd turn around and, slightly mischievously, stare at us with his little macadamia face. Look at him, Lía said, they've got him wearing a tie. Hello, handsome, she said to him, and the boy, blushing, grabbed hold of his mother.

The murmur of the audience died down. A man had clambered up onstage and was smiling smugly as he presented an aberrant biography of the Serbian pianist that he'd most likely only just memorized. He said that Mr. Rakić was from Belfast, had studied under Bazar Lerman in New York, and was now living in Italy. The audience—ever cowardly, as a stuttering friend of mine once put it—applauded all the same.

Milan emerged and sat straight down at the piano. He remained silent, with his head bowed, hands on his thighs, and maybe his eyes closed, although given the distance and the way that his straight hair hung down over his face like a black curtain, I couldn't be sure. But that was how it looked. I thought at first he was waiting for people to be quiet, but then, after the quiet had come, I thought maybe he was reviewing in his mind all the pieces he was going to play (there weren't any scores), but after that, when more than a minute had passed and people, somewhat perplexed, began looking around, I thought maybe he'd just awakened and had a filthy hangover and couldn't remember a thing, neither how to play the piano nor what the hell he was doing in a ruin in Guatemala, and least of all why he might have abandoned his beloved Belfast.

The piano began to trickle like water in a slow cascade.

Too gentle and sweet, too serene for the Chopin mazurka the program notes claimed it to be. Lía squeezed my arm. It's Beethoven's *Pathétique* she whispered, frowning, holding the piece of paper up to her face and then moving it away, hoping, I suppose, that the words would change with the angle of light, like a hologram. I shrugged, resigning myself to it. I think Milan was playing the third movement, but it could just as easily have been the second or the first. A woman to my right seemed to have fallen asleep. The boy in front was standing on his chair, listening with the genuine surprise of a child still young enough to let people dress him up in a little tie. He shouted something at his mom. She tried in vain to make him sit down. Lía smiled. For some reason, Beethoven's sonatas always make me feel like changing the world, or at least changing out of my own world. I closed my eyes for a time and imagined all the rings on Milan's pallid fingers pounding the ivory. Then silence. A round of applause. I opened my eyes and found the boy looking at me, curious, steady, barely blinking. You scare him, Lía said. I made a face like a wild leopard and he almost fell off his chair.

Head bowed, Milan had placed his hands on his thighs and again possibly had his eyes closed. Observing him in this state of deep concentration took me back to that part in his anecdote about the rainy day with the old Jew. He's deciding what to play, I whispered to Lía, who was still trying to decipher the program. Saint-Saëns, it says here. It'll be anything but Saint-Saëns, I assured her. How do you know? Bazar Lerman, I said, and just then, as if invoked by the hushed prayer of a necromancer, a gray or possibly gray-white pigeon flew into the ruins and made its way to the vault's highest point, directly above the stage.

A number of chicks began to screech while the pigeon beat her wings and tried to steady herself. Birdies! the boy shouted, already up on his feet again, pointing at his latest discovery. The audience shifted, embarrassed, and then, irrefutably, up surged Rachmaninoff. It could have been the Piano Sonata no. 2, but equally it could have been any other concerto or prelude for piano. Fast. Intense. Perfectly ordered. Like the unstoppable zephyr of a hurricane or of Lía's raging sea, I thought (or maybe felt). Then, seeing the boy's euphoria at the racket being made by the hungry chicks, I thought the music was exactly like a churning swarm of doves or parakeets or blue Amazonian cockatoos, an overcast sky full of blue Amazonian cockatoos flying gently along, screeching with a precise logic that from afar seems so chaotic, so bold, so movingly fortuitous. Milan's hands were a smudge of skin in motion. Out of focus. His hair buffeting around. The boy carried on pointing toward the roof as he hopped up and down on his metal chair: Birdies, birdies! The chicks had just then gone quiet.

Applause. Milan with his head bowed once more and another long silence. What next? murmured Lía. I didn't say anything. The program was now lying on the ground.

He started playing a forceful, energetic piece that had moments of fading to almost nothing and then, intensely, dramatically, shot upward again. An unrecognizable rise and fall that went on and on for thirty or forty minutes perhaps. But in the midst of this din of opposing emotions, of periods of peace and periods of anxiety that seemed to awaken the drowsy, ingenuous audience, I thought I heard—briefly, from a long way down, and as if tangled up in lots of other chords—a number of Thelonious Monk's syncopated melodies. Strange, I know. I thought I heard "Straight, No Chaser" and then "Trinkle, Tinkle" and then "Blue Monk" and later maybe even a small segment of "Epistrophy." Very far off. You might almost say subliminally, but not even that. Segments too fleeting to pin down, I suppose, but clear enough (within that labyrinth) for a devotee of Monk's works and particularly of his percussive style, of the way in which he used to hammer and punish the keys. Although who knows, really. Sometimes, when confusion reigns, you can only hear the music that's already inside you.

Milan vanished without a word. The people were on their feet, applauding and smiling serenely and begging for more. Clearly, he wouldn't be coming back on.

We found him in an ad hoc dressing room: on his own, smoking, a light blue towel around his neck. Lía kissed him on both cheeks. I embraced him. I don't know why, but he had the air of a wounded soldier, not fatally wounded, but vitally wounded, happily wounded, buoyantly wounded, contentedly wounded, wounded in such a way that finally he'd be able to abandon the war and go back to the peace and quiet of his home. Right, he said, stubbing out his cigarette, should we go get some food?

Lía needed to rest, she said, sleep for a few hours, but she'd join us after lunch for a coffee, she promised, and say goodbye to Milan before he made his way to the airport. He was flying back to New York that night.

We went to La Cueva de los Urquizú—a rustic, basic eatery with plastic tablecloths, plastic trays, and disposable cutlery that was probably never disposed of—so Milan could get a taste of Guatemalan food.

What's this music? he asked as he was sitting down. I told him it was a ranchera song and Milan frowned, although I had no idea why. It was dog-day hot. I ordered two beers and we began a liturgy of smoking. On one side of us, an entire family was rushing through their meal ravenously, barely even looking at one another. Živeli, said Milan, raising his beer. Salud.

I asked if he always decided what pieces to play at the last minute. Always. But please don't ask me how I decide. I don't know. Sometimes they threaten not to pay me, and once, in Rome, they even insulted and booed me, he said rather proudly, but audiences are in general tolerant or maybe they're a little innocent and they put up with my whims anyhow. You improvise, I said, depending on whether it's raining or not. Something like that, he said, smiling. I asked about the last piece. Liszt, he said, but a Liszt piece even Liszt experts don't know. I looked at him, perplexed. I played it to Berman, or Lerman, as they call him round here, and he admitted he'd never heard it before. I found it (or maybe he said discovered or rescued it). It was hidden away, gathering dust in a library in Belgrade.

The waiter came, and Milan, between sips, said you decide. To start, I ordered portions of guacamole, black beans topped with cheese, chorizo, and tortillas.

Actually, he said after a moment of quiet, it's an arrangement by Liszt for organ and later by Busoni for piano, from an opera by the German, Meyerbeer. But a strong arrangement, dark, beautiful, and one that for some reason no one knows about.

The waiter served us a number of dishes and Milan began picking at everything, freely, not asking questions, not putting out his cigarette, and not mentioning Monk.

And why such an affinity with Liszt, Milan? He looked up at me and remained quiet for a moment, but it was a bustling sort of quiet, weighted, like the portentous silence just before a train arrives. He opened his mouth but then quickly shut it again—thinking better of it, I suppose. We both watched the family of gluttons leaving slowly. Oh I don't know, he suddenly whispered in a mentholated voice, maybe because Liszt still allows for improvisation. This was what Milan said, though I'm sure there was something else he wanted to tell me. His music is an open structure, that's one way of putting it, he said, and took an immense bite out of his tortilla, which was piled high with guacamole. I suspect, he said, still chewing, it's like being able to play and stretch and fly inside a framework made of air. Hearing this, I imagined thousands of little musical notes floating around inside a white cloud, bumping into one another, desperately wanting to escape. Liszt's works allow for that, he said, much more than other composers. Know what I mean? The musician, he said, cannot be an automaton. There are boundaries laid down somewhere that at the same time aren't really there or shouldn't really be there. For instance, boundaries within a piece, or boundaries between interpretative techniques, or even boundaries between genres. Why create boundaries between genres? Why differentiate between one type of music and another? It's all the same. Music's music. And he took an endless swig of beer. Should we order something else? he said with the look of a famished, mischievous adventurer, and so I ordered a dish of pepián stew, another of caquic, and two chipilín tamales.

Sure, Milan, I said without really understanding what he was talking about, or perhaps understanding too well. But why are you so keen to push these boundaries, ignore them, make them disappear? Why are you so interested in the music of someone who invites you to move them and make them disappear? It's revolutionary. It's seditious. It's a bit bohemian, I said, in the strictest sense of that overused word. Why not work within those boundaries? Why the stubborn need to avoid them or rebel against them? Milan said nothing, swirling what was left of his beer around in the glass. Forgive the inquisition, I said, not knowing exactly where I was headed, but I'm fascinated by internal rather than external revolutions. I'm obsessed by them. For example, I'm far more interested in the motorcycle journey Che Guevara embarked on when he was twenty-four—where so many of his ideas were formed and where something magical incubated inside him for the first time—than I am by all the revolutions he went on to foment in Latin America and Africa. Up to a certain point, how and why someone is pushed toward a revolution of the spirit, whether it be artistic or social or whatever, strikes me as a far more honest search than all of the spectacle that follows. Because everything after that, Milan, is pure spectacle. Everything. Painting a canvas? Spectacle. Writing a novel? Spectacle. Playing the piano? Spectacle. And the Cuban revolution? Pure spectacle. The waiter came with our food, but I ignored him. Anyway, I said, sighing a hazy conclusion.

Milan was looking at me angrily, or at least it seemed that way: about to throw beer in my face and roar Serbian insults or perhaps burst into tears. I served myself a mountain of white rice and began covering it with big ladlefuls of spicy pepián.

Do you know what my father does? he asked me, sitting back and crossing his arms, looking like a great leader who doesn't know he's been overthrown. He was clearly nervous. I put my spoon down and sat staring at him. He's an accordionist, he said. I'm the son of a Gypsy accordionist, he said, and finished his beer. Waiter, he called, lifting his bottle, two more. He smiled ironically. And your mother? I asked. He shook his head with an air of shame or bitterness. Only my father is a Gypsy. Not my mother. I look more like her, I mean, my features are more Serbian than Gypsy. I didn't say anything. I didn't know what to say. For as long as I can remember my father has fought to keep me as far away as possible from both his world and his music, to keep them from me. But, like you said yesterday about jazz, I've got Gypsy music deep in my gonads. I could have sworn, given the menace in the way he said it, that Milan was grabbing or at least stroking his gonads under the table. I never bring any Liszt CDs on any of my trips, no Chopin, no Rachmaninoff. But I can't go a single day, Eduardito, without hearing a bit of Gypsy music, a bit of Boban Marković, or Oláh Vince, or the legendary Šaban Bajramović. He smiled. Deep down, I'm a nomad, like them, even if my father wants to deny it. And a nomad doesn't much like boundaries. Ah, he said to the waiter, thanks very much, and took a sip of beer. Imagine, he went on, as if gripped by some terrible inertia. I've been sitting at the piano for twenty-five years, studying with the best classical teachers in the best schools in the world, and all I dream about is being among Gypsies, playing and dancing and feeling the pain of their music. Ridiculous, isn't it? Milan began serving himself generous spoonfuls of pepián and caquic, and I, considering him brave to attempt such a mixture, could only think about how some people flee their ancestors, while others yearn for them, almost viscerally; how a few run from their fathers' world, while others clamor for it, cry out for it; how I couldn't get far enough away from Judaism, while Milan would never be close enough to the Gypsies. And your father? I asked, sensing the answer. He doesn't know, he said without looking up, his gaze lost in pieces of carrots and squash and goodness knows what else. He can't know. Milan cut a chunk out of one of the little chipilín tamales with his fork and then, as if I were some watered-down version of his father, confessed: I want to give up classical music. Neither of us said a word, and we finished the food and the beers in that drawn-out silence, exhausted by all the talk, or maybe just allowing all those words to finally find their mark.

We ordered flan and coffee. Suddenly—I don't know whether out of sincerity or impertinence—I said I wanted to know more about Gypsies, about their music, and Milan just said sure, with a disdainful flick of his head. How did you get on last night? I asked. And lighting a cigarette and raising his eyebrows with the mischievous air of a teenage troubadour, he asked me if all Mayan girls liked to fuck standing up.

White Smoke

When I met her in a Scottish bar, after I don't know how many beers and almost an entire pack of unfiltered Camels, she told me that she liked it when men bit her nipples, and hard.

It wasn't actually a Scottish bar, just some old bar in Antigua, Guatemala, that only served beer and was called (or was referred to as) the Scottish bar. I was drinking a Moza at the counter. I prefer dark beer. It makes me think of old-fashioned taverns and sword fights. I lit a cigarette and she asked me in English, sitting on a stool to my right, if I'd give her one. I guessed from her accent that she was Israeli. Bevakasha, I said to her, which means you're welcome in Hebrew, and I held out the box of matches. She got friendly right away. She said something to me in Hebrew that I didn't understand and I clarified that I really remembered only three or four words and a random prayer or two and maybe how to count to ten. Fifteen, if I really tried. I live in the capital, I told her in Spanish, to show that I wasn't an American, and she admitted that she was confused because she hadn't imagined there were any Jewish Guatemalans. I'm not Jewish anymore, I said, smiling at her, I retired. What do you mean you're not? That's impossible, she yelled in that way Israelis have of yelling. She turned toward me. She was wearing a thin white Indian-style cotton blouse, torn jeans, and yellow espadrilles. Her hair was dark brown and she had emerald blue eyes, if emerald blue even exists. She explained to me that she had recently finished her military service, that she was traveling around Central America with her friend, and that they had decided to stay in Antigua for a few weeks to take Spanish classes and make a little money. With her, she said, pointing to show me. Yael. Her friend, a pale, serious girl with exquisite shoulders, had served me the beer. I greeted her while they spoke in Hebrew, laughing, and I thought I heard them mention the number seven at one point, but I'm not sure why. A German couple came in and her friend went to serve them. She grabbed my hand firmly, told me it was a pleasure to meet me, that her name was Tamara, and then took another one of my cigarettes, this time without asking.

I ordered a second beer and Yael brought us two Mozas and a plate of chips. She stayed where she was, standing in front of us. I asked Tamara her last name. I remember that it was Russian. Halfon is Lebanese, I said, but my mother's last name, Tenenbaum, is Polish, from Łódź, and both girls shrieked. It turned out that Yael's last name was also Tenenbaum, and while she verified it on my driver's license, I started to think about the remote possibility that we were related, and I imagined a novel about two Polish siblings who thought their entire family had been exterminated but who all of a sudden find each other after sixty years apart, thanks to the grandchildren, a Guatemalan writer and an Israeli hippie, who meet by chance in a Scottish bar that isn't even Scottish in Antigua, Guatemala. Yael got a liter of cheap beer and filled three glasses. Tamara gave me my license back and the three of us drank a toast to us, to them, to the Poles. We stayed silent, listening to an old Bob Marley song and contemplating the immense smallness of the planet.

Tamara picked up my lit cigarette from the ashtray, took a long drag, and asked me what I did for a living. I told her seriously that I was a pediatrician and a professional liar. She raised her hand like a stop sign. I liked her hand a lot, and I don't know why, but I remembered a line of poetry by e. e. cummings that Woody Allen quotes in one of his movies about infidelity. Nobody, I told her while I trapped her hand like a pale and fragile butterfly, not even the rain, has such small hands. Tamara smiled, told me that her parents were doctors and that she also wrote poems once in a while, and I supposed that she had attributed e. e. cummings's line to me, but I didn't feel like correcting her. And she didn't let go of my hand.

Yael filled our glasses while I clumsily smoked with my left hand and they spoke in Hebrew. What happened? I asked Tamara, and with a sorrowful pout she told me that the day before someone had robbed her. She sighed. I walked all morning, through the artisan market, by some ruins, everywhere, and when I sat down on a bench in the central park (that's what the Antiguans call it, even though it's really a square), I realized that someone had cut my bag with a knife. She explained to me that she had lost some money and some papers. Yael said something in Hebrew and they both laughed. What? I asked, curious, but they kept laughing and speaking in Hebrew. I squeezed Tamara's hand and she remembered that I was there and told me that the money didn't matter as much as the papers. I asked her what papers they were. She smiled enigmatically, like a Dutch tulip seller. Four hits of acid, she murmured in her poor Spanish. I took a drink of beer. You like acid? she asked me, and I told her that I didn't know, that I had never tried it. Tamara, euphoric, in her element, talked to me for ten or twenty minutes about how necessary acid is to open our minds and make us more tolerant and peaceful people, and the only thing I could think about while she chattered on was ripping her clothes off right there, in front of Yael and the German couple and any other Scottish voyeur who might want to spy on us. In order to stop her and also to relax a little, I suppose, I lit a cigarette and held it out to her. The first time I tried acid, she said while we passed the cigarette back and forth, was with my friends in Tel Aviv, and I got all sleepy, and very, very relaxed, and I think I saw God. I seem to remember that she said Dios, in Spanish, although she also could have said Hashem or God or maybe G–d, the way Jewish people write God so as not to take his name in vain—in case they rip the paper it's written on, I guess. I didn't know if I should laugh and so I just asked her what God's face looked like. He didn't have a face, she replied. So what did you see? She told me that it was difficult to explain, and then she closed her eyes, taking on a mystical air, waiting for some divine revelation. I don't believe in God, I told her, waking her from her trance, but I do talk to him every day. She got serious. You don't consider yourself a Jew and you don't believe in God? she asked me reproachfully, and I just shrugged and said what for, and then went to the bathroom without giving any more time to such a useless topic.

While I was taking a piss, I noticed that, in spite of being a little drunk, I already had a slight erection. Then I washed my hands, thinking about my grandfather, about Auschwitz, about the five green digits tattooed on his fore-arm, which for all of my childhood I thought were there, as he used to tell me himself, so that he could remember his telephone number. And without knowing why, I felt a bit guilty.

I came back from the bathroom. I could hear Bob Dylan's raspy voice. Tamara was singing. Yael had filled my glass up again and was flirting with a guy who seemed Scottish and was very possibly the owner of the bar. I sat watching Yael. She had a silver belly-button ring. I imagined her in mili-tary uniform, carrying a huge machine gun. I turned back and saw that Tamara was smiling at me while she sang. I could only imagine her naked.

I took a long drink until the glass was empty. An old campesino had come in to the bar and was trying to sell ma-chetes and huipiles. I told Tamara that I was already late for a meeting but that we could get together the next day. Can you come from the capital? she asked. Of course, gladly, it's a thirty-minute drive. All right, she said. I get out of class at six. Should we meet here again? Ken, I said to her, which means yes in Hebrew, and I half-smiled. I love your mouth, it's shaped like a heart, she said, and grazed my lips with her finger. I said thank you, and told her that I loved when women grazed my lips with their fingers. Me too, Tamara murmured in her bad Spanish, and then, still in Spanish and baring her teeth like a hungry lioness, she added: But I like it better when men bite my nipples, and hard. I didn't understand if she knew exactly what she was saying or if she was joking. She leaned toward me and I got chills when she gave me a soft kiss on my neck. With a shudder, I wondered what her nipples would look like, round or pointed, pink or red or maybe translucent violet, and standing up, I told her in Spanish that that was a shame, that when I do bite them, I bite them softly.

I paid for all the beers and we agreed to meet there the following evening, at six o'clock. I hugged her tightly, feeling something that couldn't be named but that was as thick and distinct as the white smoke of the Vatican on a dark winter night, and knowing very well that the next day I wouldn't be coming back.

The Polish Boxer

69752. That it was his phone number. That he had it tattooed there, on his left forearm, so he wouldn't forget it. That's what my grandfather told me. And that's what I grew up believing. In the 1970s, telephone numbers in Guatemala were five digits long.

I called him Oitze, because he called me Oitze, which means something soppy in Yiddish. I liked his Polish accent. I liked dipping my pinkie (the only physical feature I inherited from him: these two curved little fingers, more warped every day) in his glass of whiskey. I liked asking him to draw me pictures, but he only actually knew how to draw one picture, quickly sketched, always identical, of a sinuous and disfigured hat. I liked the beet-red color of the sauce (chrain, in Yiddish) that he poured over his white ball of fish (gefilte fish, in Yiddish). I liked going with him on his walks around the neighborhood, the same neighborhood where one night, in the middle of a big vacant lot, a planeful of cows had crashed. But most of all I liked that number. His number.

It didn't take me too long, however, to understand his telephone joke, and the psychological importance of that joke, and eventually, although nobody would admit it, the historical origin of that number. Then, when we went for walks together or he started drawing a series of hats, I would stare at those five digits and, strangely happy, play a game of inventing secret scenes of how he might have gotten them. My grandfather faceup on a hospital bed while, straddling him, an enormous German officer (dressed in black leather) shouted out the numbers one at a time to an anemic-looking German nurse (also dressed in black leather), who then handed him, one by one, the hot irons. Or my grandfather sitting on a wooden bench in front of a semicircle of Germans in white coats and white gloves, with white lights fastened around their heads, like miners, when suddenly one of the Germans stammered out a number and a clown rode in on a unicycle and all the lights shone their white light on my grandfather while the clown—with a big green marker, in ink that could never be erased—wrote that number on his forearm, and all the German scientists applauded. Or my grandfather standing at the ticket booth of a cinema, sticking his left arm in through the little round opening in the glass where they pass you the tickets, and on the other side of the window, a fat, hairy German woman setting the five digits on one of those stamps with adjustable dates like they use in banks (the same kind of stamps my dad kept on the desk in his office and that I liked to play with), and then, as if it was an extremely important date, stamping it hard and forever onto my grandfather's forearm.

That's how I played with his number. Clandestinely. Hypnotized by those five mysterious green digits that, much more than on his forearm, seemed to me to be tattooed on some part of his soul.

Green and mysterious until not so long ago.

In the late afternoon, sitting on his old butter-colored leather sofa, I was drinking whiskey with my grandfather.

I noticed that the green wasn't as green as it used to be, but more of a diluted, pale, grayish color that made me think of something decomposing. The 7 had almost amalgamated with the 5. The 6 and the 9, unrecognizable, were now two swollen blobs, deformed and out of focus. The 2, in full flight, gave the impression of having moved a few millimeters away from the rest of them. I looked at my grandfather's face and suddenly realized that in my childhood game, in each of my boyish fantasies, I had imagined him already old, already a grandfather. As if he'd been born a grandfather, or as if he'd aged once and for all at the very moment of receiving that number, which I was now examining so meticulously.

It was in Auschwitz.

At first, I wasn't sure I'd heard him. I looked up. He was covering the number with his right hand. Drizzle purred against the roof tiles.

This, he said, rubbing his forearm gently. It was in Auschwitz, he said. It was with the boxer, he said without looking at me and with no emotion whatsoever and speaking in an accent no longer his own.

I would have liked to ask him what it felt like when, after almost sixty years of silence, he finally said something truthful about the origin of that number. Ask him why he had said it to me. Ask him if releasing words so long stored up produced some liberating effect. Ask him if words stored up for so long had the same taste as they rolled roughly off the tongue. But I kept quiet, impatient, listening to the rain, fearing something, perhaps the intense transcendence of the moment, perhaps that he might not tell me anything more, perhaps that the true story behind those five digits might not be as fantastic as all my childhood versions.

Oitze, pour me another drop, eh, he said, handing me his glass.

I did, knowing that if my grandmother came back early from her errands, I'd be in trouble. Since he started having heart problems, my grandfather drank two ounces of whiskey at midday and another two ounces before supper. No more. Except on special occasions, of course, like a party or wedding or soccer match or a television appearance by Isabel Pantoja. But I thought he was building up strength for what he wanted to tell me. Then I thought that, by having more to drink than he should in his current state of health, telling me what he wanted to tell could upset him, possibly too much. He leaned back on the old sofa and savored that first sweet sip, and I remembered one time when, as a kid, I heard him tell my grandmother that she needed to buy more Red Label, the only whiskey he drank, even though I had recently discovered more than thirty bottles stored away in the cellar. Brand new. And I told him so. And my grandfather answered with a smile full of mystery, with wisdom full of some kind of pain I would never understand: In case there's a war, Oitze.

He was sort of gone. His eyes were glazed over, fixed on the big window, through which we could contemplate the crests of rain falling over almost the whole of the green immensity of the Colonia Elgin ravine. He was chewing on something, a seed or a little bit of grit, perhaps. Then I noticed the top button of his gabardine pants was undone and his fly half-open.

I was at Sachsenhausen concentration camp. Near Berlin. From November of '39.

And he licked his lips quite a bit, as if what he'd just said was edible. He was still covering the number with his right hand while, with the left, he held the whiskey glass. I picked up the bottle and asked him if he wanted me to pour him a little more, but he didn't answer or perhaps he didn't hear.

In Sachsenhausen, near Berlin, he continued, there were two blocks of Jewish prisoners and lots of blocks of German prisoners, maybe fifty blocks of Germans, lots of German prisoners, German thieves and German murderers and Germans who'd married Jewish women. Rassenschande, they called it in German. Racial shame.

He was quiet again, and it seemed to me that his speech was like a calm surge. Maybe because memory is also pendular. Maybe because pain can be tolerated only in measured doses. I wanted to ask him to talk to me about Łódź and his brothers and sisters and parents (he had one family photo, only one, that he'd obtained many years later from an uncle who'd emigrated before the war broke out, and which he kept hanging on the wall by his bed, and which didn't make me feel anything, as if those pale faces weren't of real people, but the gray and anonymous faces of characters torn from some history textbook), ask him to talk to me about everything that had happened to him before '39, before Sachsenhausen.

The rain let up a little and a swollen white cloud began to climb out of the depths of the ravine.

I was the stubendienst of our block. The one in charge

of our block. Three hundred men. Two hundred and eighty men. Three hundred and ten men. Every day a few more, every day a few less. You see, Oitze, he said as an affirmation, not a question, and I thought he was making sure of my presence, of my company, as if he didn't want to be left alone with those words. He said, and put invisible food to his lips: I was in charge of getting them coffee in the mornings and later, in the afternoons, potato soup and a piece of bread. He said, and fanned the air with his hand: I was in charge of cleaning, of sweeping, of changing the cots. He said, and kept fanning the air with his hand: I was in charge of removing the bodies of the men who were dead in the mornings. He said, almost announcing: But I was also in charge of receiving the new Jews when they arrived in my block, when they shouted Juden eintreffen, Juden eintreffen, and I went out to meet them and I realized that almost all the Jews who came into my block had some valuable object hidden on them. A little necklace or a watch, a ring or a diamond. Something. Well hidden. Well tucked away somewhere. Sometimes they'd swallowed these objects, and then a day or two later they would come out in their shit.

He held out his glass and I poured him another shot of whiskey.

It was the first time I'd ever heard my grandfather say shit, and the word, at that moment, in that context, seemed beautiful.

Why you, Oitze? I asked him, taking advantage of a brief silence. He frowned and closed his eyes a little and stared at me as if we suddenly spoke different languages. Why did they put you in charge?

And on his old face, in his old hand, which had now stopped gesturing and gone back to covering up the number, I saw all the implications of that question. I saw the disguised question inside that question: What did you have to do for them to put you in charge? I saw the question that is never asked: What did you have to do to survive?

He smiled, shrugging his shoulders.

One day, our lagerleiter, the camp commander, just told me that I'd be in charge, and that was it.

As if you could speak the unspeakable.

Though a long time before, he went on after a sip, in '39, when I'd just arrived at Sachsenhausen, near Berlin, our lagerleiter found me one morning hidden under the cot. I didn't want to go and work, you see, and I thought I could stay all day hidden under the cot. I don't know how, but the lagerleiter found me hidden under the cot and dragged me outside and started beating me here, at the base of my spine, with a wooden or maybe an iron rod. I don't know how many times. Until I passed out. I was in bed for ten or twelve days, unable to walk. From then on, the lagerleiter changed the way he treated me. He said good morning and good afternoon to me. He told me he liked how clean I kept my cot. And one day he told me I'd be the stubendienst, the one in charge of cleaning my block. Just like that.

He sat pensively, shaking his head.

I don't remember his name, or his face, he said, then chewed something a couple of times, turned to one side to spit it out, and as if that absolved him, as if that might be enough, added: He had very elegant hands.

I should have known. My grandfather kept his own hands impeccable. Once a week, sitting in front of the increasingly loud television, my grandmother removed his cuticles with little tweezers, cut and filed his nails, and then, while she did the same to the other hand, he soaked them in a tiny dish full of a slimy transparent liquid that smelled like varnish. When both hands were done, she took a blue tin of Nivea and spread and massaged the white cream into each of his fingers, slowly, gently, until both hands had absorbed it completely, and my grandfather would then put the black stone ring back on the little finger of his right hand, where he'd worn it for almost sixty years, as a sign of mourning.

All the Jews gave me those objects they brought in secretly when they entered Sachsenhausen, near Berlin. You see. Since I was in charge. And I took those objects and negotiated in secret with the Polish cooks and obtained something even more valuable for the Jews who were coming in. I exchanged a watch for an extra piece of bread. A gold chain for a bit more coffee. A diamond for the last ladleful of soup in the pot, where the only two or three potatoes had always sunk.

The murmur on the roof tiles started up again and I began to think of those two or three insipid, overcooked potatoes that, in a world demarcated by barbed wire, were so much more valuable than the most splendid diamond.

One day, I decided to give the lagerleiter a twenty-dollar gold coin.

I took out my cigarettes and started toying with one. I could say I didn't light it out of sorrow, out of respect for my grandfather, out of courtesy for that twenty-dollar gold coin, which I immediately imagined black and rusty. But I'd better not.

I decided to give a twenty-dollar gold coin to the lagerleiter. Maybe I thought I'd earned his trust, or maybe I wanted to get on his good side. One day, there was a Ukrainian among the group of Jews who came in, and he slipped me a twenty-dollar gold coin. The Ukrainian had smuggled it in under his tongue. Days and days with a twenty-dollar gold coin hidden under his tongue, and the Ukrainian handed it over to me, and I waited until everyone had left the block and gone out to the fields to work and then I went to the lagerleiter and gave it to him. The lagerleiter didn't say a word. He simply put it into the top pocket of his jacket, turned around, and walked away. A few days later, I was awakened by a kick to the gut. They pushed me outside, and the lagerleiter was standing there, wearing a black raincoat and with his hands behind his back, and then I reacted and understood why they kept punching and kicking me. There was snow on the ground. No one spoke. They threw me in the back of a truck and closed the door, and I was half-dozing and shivering the whole way. It was daytime when the truck finally stopped. Through a crack in the wood I could see the big sign over the metal gate. Arbeit Macht Frei, it said. Work shall set you free. I heard laughter. But cynical laughter, you see, dirty laughter, mocking me with that stupid sign. Someone opened the back of the truck. They ordered me to get out. There was snow everywhere. I saw the Black Wall. Then I saw Block Eleven. It was '42 by then and we'd all heard about Block Eleven at Auschwitz. We knew that people who went into Block Eleven at Auschwitz never came out. They threw me into a cell and left me there, lying on the floor in Block Eleven in Auschwitz.

In a futile but somehow necessary gesture, my grandfather lifted his glass, now empty of whiskey, to his lips.

It was a dark cell. Very damp. With a low ceiling. There was hardly any light at all. Or air. Just damp. And people piled up. Lots of people piled up. Some people crying. Other people murmuring the Kaddish.

I lit my cigarette.

My grandfather used to say that I was the same age as traffic lights, because the first traffic light in Guatemala had been installed at some intersection downtown the very day I was born. Idling in front of a traffic light was also where I asked my mother how babies got into women's tummies. I was half-kneeling on the backseat of an enormous jade-colored Volvo that, for some reason, vibrated when it stopped at traffic lights. I didn't mention that a friend (Hasbun) had confidentially told us during recess that a woman got pregnant when a man gave her a kiss on the lips, and another friend (Asturias) had argued, much more audaciously, that a man and a woman had to take off all their clothes together and then shower together and then even sleep together in the same bed, without having to touch each other. I stood in that wonderful space between the backseat and the two front seats and waited for an answer. The Volvo vibrated before a red light on Vista Hermosa Boulevard, the sky entirely blue, the smell of tobacco and aniseed chewing gum, the black and sugary look of a campesino in rough sandals who came over to beg for change, my mother's embarrassed silence as she tried to find some words, these words: Well, when a woman wants a baby, she goes to the doctor and he gives her a blue pill if she wants a little boy and a pink pill if she wants a little girl, and then she takes the pill and that's it, she gets pregnant. The light turned green. The Volvo stopped vibrating and I, still standing and holding on to whatever I could so I wouldn't go flying, imagined myself stuck in a glass jar, all mixed up among blue little boys and pink little girls, my name engraved in bas-relief (just like the name Bayer on the aspirins I had to take sometimes and that tasted so much like plaster), still and silent as I waited for some lady to arrive at the doctor's clinic (I saw her wide and distorted through the glass, like in one of those undulating mirrors at the circus) and swallow me with a little water (and with the ingenuous perception of a child, of course, I perceived the cruelty of chance, the casual violence that would toss me into the open hand of some woman, any woman, a big, sweaty, fortuitous hand that would then throw me into a mouth just as big, sweaty, and fortuitous) in order, finally, to introduce me into an unknown tummy so that I could be born. I've never been able to shake off the feeling of solitude and abandonment I felt stuck in that glass jar. Sometimes I forget it, or perhaps decide to forget it, or perhaps, absurdly, assure myself that I've completely forgotten it. Until something, anything, the slightest thing, sticks me back into that glass jar. For example: my first sexual encounter, at the age of fifteen, with a prostitute in a five-peso brothel called El Puente. For example: a mistaken room at the end of a trip to the Balkans. For example: a yellow canary that, in the middle of a square in Tecpán, chose a secret and pink prophecy. For example: the last icy handshake from a stuttering friend. For example: the claustrophobic image of the dark, damp, crowded cell stuffed with whispers where my grandfather was locked up, sixty years ago, in Block Eleven, in Auschwitz.

People crying and people saying Kaddish.

I brought over the ashtray. I felt a little light-headed, but I poured us the rest of the whiskey anyway.

What else have you got left when you know the next day you're going to be shot, eh? Nothing. You either lie down and cry or you lie down and say Kaddish. I didn't know the Kaddish. But that night, for the first time in my life, I also said Kaddish. I said Kaddish thinking of my parents and I said Kaddish thinking that the next day I'd be shot kneeling in front of the Black Wall of Auschwitz. It was '42 by then and we'd all heard of the Black Wall at Auschwitz and I had seen the Black Wall with my own eyes as I got out of the truck and knew perfectly well that was where they shot people. Gnadenschuss, a single shot to the back of the neck. But the Black Wall of Auschwitz didn't look as big as I'd imagined. It didn't look as black, either. It was black, with little white pockmarks. It had white pockmarks all over it, said my grandfather while pressing invisible aerial keys with his index finger, and I, smoking, imagined a starry sky. He said: Splashes of white. He said: Made by the very bullets that had gone through the backs of so many necks.

It was very dark in the cell, he went on quickly, as if not to get lost in that same darkness. And a man sitting beside me began to speak to me in Polish. Maybe he heard me saying Kaddish and recognized my accent. He was a Jew from Łódź. We were both Jews from Łódź, but I was from Żeromskiego Street, near the Źielony Rynek market, and he was from the opposite side, near Poniatowskiego Park. He was a boxer from Łódź. A Polish boxer. And we talked all night in Polish. Or rather, he talked to me all night in Polish. He told me in Polish that he had been there for a long time, in Block Eleven, and that the Germans kept him alive because they liked to watch him box. He told me in Polish that the next day they'd put me on trial and he told me in Polish what I should say during that trial and what I shouldn't say during that trial. And that's how it went. The next day, two Germans dragged me out of the cell, took me to a young Jewish man, who tattooed this number on my arm, and then they left me in an office, where I was put on trial by a young woman, and I saved myself by telling this young woman everything the Polish boxer had told me to say and not telling the young woman everything the Polish boxer had told me not to say. You see? I used his words and his words saved my life and I never knew the Polish boxer's name, never saw his face. He was probably shot.

I stubbed out my cigarette in the ashtray and downed the last sip of whiskey. I wanted to ask him something about the number or about that young Jewish man who had tattooed him. But I only asked what the Polish boxer had said. He seemed not to understand my question, and so I repeated it, a bit louder, a bit more anxiously. What did the boxer tell you to say and not say, Oitze, during that trial?

My grandfather laughed, still confused, and leaned back, and I remembered that he refused to speak Polish, that he had spent sixty years refusing to speak a single word in his mother tongue, in the mother tongue of those who, in November of '39, he always said, had betrayed him.

I never found out if my grandfather didn't remember the Polish boxer's words, or if he chose not to tell them to me, or if they simply didn't matter anymore, if they had now served their purpose as words and so had disappeared forever, along with the Polish boxer who spoke them one dark night.

Once more, I sat looking at my grandfather's number, 69752, tattooed one winter morning in '42, by a young Jew in Auschwitz. I tried to imagine the face of the Polish boxer, imagine his fists, imagine the possible white pockmark the bullet had made after going through his neck, imagine his words in Polish that managed to save my grandfather's life, but all I could imagine was an endless line of individuals, all naked, all pale, all thin, all weeping or saying Kaddish in absolute silence, all devout believers in a religion whose faith is based on numbers, as they waited in line to be numbered themselves.

Postcards

The naked isle. That's how Milan titled the first postcard I received. Two acrobatic dolphins leaped in the foreground, inviting me to come visit them in some aquatic park in Florida. Milan had filled the blank space on the back of the huge card (maybe half a letter-size page) with microscopic print, so minuscule and scrunched up that the whole text looked as if it had been written by a child. A skilled child, but a child nonetheless.

Gypsy singer Šaban Bajramović was born in the Yugoslav city of Niš in 1936. At age eighteen he deserted from Tito's army, and as a result the communist authorities sent him to Goli Otok, which means the naked isle: a giant, desolate rock on the Dalmatian coast where the prisoners died of dehydration, from so much sun, so much neglect. Šaban Bajramović had deserted the Yugoslav army for a woman. He managed to survive a year on Goli Otok (I am writing a letter and crying / I am dying in prison here / The years pass, flying / And they are not freeing me). There, on that rock, he learned to write. The other prisoners called him Black Panther. The other prisoners slashed his face and nearly disemboweled him: a huge scar runs from his chest to his pelvis. When he was finally freed in 1964, he recorded his first songs and used the money he earned to buy himself a white suit and a white Mercedes, both of which he lost in a dart game that very same night (When I had the money, I gave it all away / And now I have no money / I have no friends / So I implore the little snail to sell me his little house). Šaban Bajramović's music is not Šaban Bajramović's music. He's never copyrighted it, never protected it. No one knows where he lives, where he's traveling. All of a sudden, he'll turn up at some Gypsy music festival in Sarajevo or maybe the Gypsy cafés in Budapest. All of a sudden, he'll disappear again. And that, my dear Eduardito, is how one of the best Gypsy singers of all time lives. As if he were still a black panther. As if he were still the sole survivor on that inhospitable naked isle. Roving around, all alone, who knows where. No ties or responsibilities or boundaries of any kind. No boundaries.

I pinned the postcard to my studio wall, dolphin side out, right between an alleged photo of a now-aged Thomas Pynchon walking the streets of New York with his son, and Lía's only orgasm sketch that wasn't done in her almond-colored notebook, a sketch that could have been of the trajectory of some South American river, with tributaries and rivulets and everything, drawn one cold rainy afternoon after we made love (placid yet uncomfortable, of course) in the bathtub.

His big obsession, Milan had told me at some point, was postcards. He liked sending postcards, not receiving them. In fact, he always refused to give me his own address. I don't have one, he said jokingly, or on second thought, perhaps seriously. He said: I live on the lungo drom, which in Romany means the long road, with no set destination and no turning back. He said: I travel in a caravan of one. He said: On the road, for my friends, I leave a trail of patrin, which in Romany means signs placed along the way, like a branch broken in a certain fashion, or a handful of twigs tied up in a blue handkerchief, or goat bones sticking out of the ground. He said: Postcards are my patrin.

Lía told me that a long time ago she'd seen a movie in which different Gypsy caravans communicated by leaving those kinds of markers along the way, markers that were interpreted as witchcraft and necromancy by the inhabitants of a small, anachronistic town in Spain. One night, when a local girl suddenly died after having played near some Gypsy markers that afternoon, the town's inhabitants became a frenzied mob and set out with torches and sickles and hacked to pieces every Gypsy they found sleeping peacefully among the trees. Men, women, and children. Lía couldn't remember whether or not that was the end of the movie, but she thought it was.

The next postcard didn't say anything, or at least it didn't say anything in writing. I knew it was from him because of the minuscule block letters my name and address were printed in. Plus, who else in their right mind still sends postcards? According to the postmark, it was sent from Washington, D.C. It was a reproduction of a Chagall painting, or perhaps just a detail from the painting. At first, I thought there was no connection between the

Chagall painting and Milan; then I thought that perhaps there was, and I spent several days trying to unravel it, to find in the image some meaning that would allude to the life of the Serbian pianist. It wasn't until much later, though, when perhaps it was already too late, that I understood what Milan, by not saying anything, had said.

I got a postcard from Denver of an horchata-colored mountain, full of tiny black dots, which I took to be conifers or possibly giant skiers. Milan wrote: Once upon a time there was a king who was in possession of the Romany alphabet. And because in those days there were no bookshelves to hold alphabets, the king wrapped it up in lettuce leaves and fell asleep beside a gently flowing stream. After a while, a donkey came along, drank a bit of water from the brook, and ate the lettuce leaves. And that's why we Gypsies have no alphabet.

I got a postcard from Boston of a bay by night, all lit up. Milan wrote: We Gypsies, Eduardito, have three great talents. Making music. Telling stories. And the third one is a secret.

Doll, in his Lilliputian block print, was how he'd entitled the next postcard, also enormous, sent from Mexico City. On the front was a collage with mariachis and tricolor flags and white sand beaches and, right smack in the middle, as though reining it all in to or radiating it all out from her beautiful golden aura, a flamboyant Virgin of Guadalupe. Milan wrote: Her real name was Bronisława Wajs, though everyone knew her by her Gypsy name, Papusza, which means doll. Like the majority of Polish Gypsies at the turn of the century, Papusza came from a family of nomads. A family of harpist nomads. When she turned fifteen, Papusza, of course, married a harpist nomad. And on her later travels, somehow, perhaps while the caravan was stopped in various settlements for a few days, or perhaps while everyone was holed up in the village until winter passed, Papusza learned to read and write. Even today, Eduardito, three out of four Gypsy women are illiterate. She wrote long ballads she called simply, "Songs from Papusza's Head." In the summer of 1949, by sheer coincidence, the Polish poet Jerzy Ficowski heard her sing and immediately began to copy and transcribe and translate some of her songs, which he published in a journal called *Problemy*. Papusza was forced to appear before Poland's highest Gypsy authority, who, after brief deliberation, deemed her mahrine, or contaminated, for having collaborated with gadje, or non-Gypsies. She was sentenced to permanent expulsion from the caravan. A few months later, Papusza was discharged from a psychiatric hospital (No one understands me / Only the forest and river / That of which I speak / Has all, all passed away / Everything, everything has gone with it / And those years of youth), and she lived out the rest of her life in the most absolute solitude and the most absolute silence. Like a marvelous fucking doll, ragged and abandoned, that ends up rotting in some box in the attic. Isn't it incredible, Eduardito, how in the end Gypsies always live up to their nicknames, as if they were providential orders or divine mandates? So what do you think my nickname will be? What will my divine mandate be? Papusza died in 1987.

Gently, with an acupuncturist's steady hand, I pinned the postcard to my studio wall.

I'd made several attempts to track Milan down. A few phone calls. A few e-mails. Always halfheartedly, of course: without really wanting to track him down. I wanted to talk to him and to ask him things, but I also wanted to respect his desire to be untrackable, unreachable, almost missing, peregrinating, with no roots or ties. He'd adopted, as far as possible, the life of a nomad, but a modern nomad, an allegorical nomad, a postcard nomad, an ululating nomad in a world where being a real nomad is now forbidden.

I got a postcard of a mauve desert dusk, sent from Arizona. Milan wrote: Many centuries ago, a Gypsy was traveling with all of his family in a covered wagon, an old covered wagon pulled by a feeble, skinny nag. The more children the Gypsy and his wife had, the harder it got for the poor nag, and the whole covered wagon lurched this way and then that, and cups and frying pans rattled, and from time to time one of the Gypsies' children went flying out of the covered wagon, barefoot. And that's how Gypsies came to be scattered all over the world. All over Europe and India and the Middle East and Africa and North America and South America and Australia and New Zealand. Millions and millions of Gypsies, Eduardito, all children fallen from that same ramshackle wagon.

I got a postcard from New York entitled Yusef. It was a black-and-white photograph (a perfect photograph, according to Lía) of four jazz musicians standing in front of the famous fifties jazz club Minton's Playhouse: Teddy Hill, Roy Eldridge, Howard McGhee and, of course, as his wife called him, Melodious Thunk, but a symbolic Melodious Thunk, if there are such things as symbols, a metaphorical Melodious Thunk, if metaphors are anything more than tiny ants crawling furiously between your toes. Milan wrote: They called him Yusef. No one knows if that was really his name or even what country he was from. The old people say listening to Yusef's accordion was like listening to a siren's sweet song. The old people say listening to Yusef's accordion was like listening to the cries of Christ on the cross. The old people say Yusef managed to survive four years in Chelmno Nazi extermination camp, on the shores of the river Ner, playing at German officers' parties every night. The old people say Yusef, night after night, played one piece for every Gypsy killed that day in the gas chamber. The old people say Yusef, during those four years, played 350,000 pieces. Twenty-five a night, more or less. The old people say when he was freed after the war, Yusef unstrapped his accordion and left it on the green grass of Chelmno.

I got a postcard of a bikinied blond with huge tits and huge lips who was straddling a Harley. Postmarked New Orleans. Milan wrote: My father says Yusef the accordionist never existed.

I got a giant postcard sent from Hawaii, though the photo, for some reason, was a cosmopolitan-looking aerial shot of the city of Philadelphia. VISIT THE CITY OF BROTHERLY LOVE said a yellow neon sign whose huge letters actually seemed to twinkle. Milan wrote: The Gypsies' origins, Eduardito, are eminently musical. This is how it happened: Around the year 428, the Gypsies arrived in Persia when Bahran Gur, the Shah, wishing to please his subjects, imported twelve thousand musicians from India. No. That's not how it happened, Eduardito. This is how it happened: One day, God put a violin on Saint Peter's shoulder. When the people began to demand that he play them a tune, Saint Peter became frightened and ran off to find God, and God calmed him by saying that he'd given him the violin so that his music might make the people happy and forever keep their spirits up. Then Saint Peter told God that if that were true, there should be many more musicians in the world. God asked him who they should be and Saint Peter, as he played a jaunty tune, replied: the Gypsies. But no, that's not how it happened either, Eduardito. This is how it happened: Once upon a time there was a very beautiful girl who was in love with a tall, strong, hardworking peasant who never noticed her. One afternoon, as the girl was walking in the forest, feeling sad and lonely, there appeared before her a huge man with purple eyes, dressed in red, with two horns on his head and hooves for feet: the devil, stroking her lips with his long, sharp nail, promised her the young peasant's love if in exchange she would give him her entire family. The girl agreed gladly. She gave the devil her father, and the devil turned him into a violin. She gave the devil her mother, and the devil turned her into the bow and her long gray locks into the bow hair. She gave the devil her four brothers, and the devil turned them into four strings. Then the devil taught the girl to play the violin, and she learned to play so sweetly and so tenderly and so beautifully that when the young peasant heard her, he immediately fell in love. And they married and lived happily together for many years. But one day, after playing and dancing in the forest, they both went off to pick raspberries and left the violin behind on the forest floor. Upon their return, they could no longer find it. Then, from a cloudy sky, the devil descended in a chariot pulled by four black horses and carried off the unlucky couple forever. For a long time, the violin lay there in the forest, hidden beneath dry leaves and moss and more dry leaves. But one night, some Gypsies camping in the forest sent a boy in search of firewood for their bonfire and, when he kicked a pile of leaves, the boy discovered the violin. He stroked it with a twig and the violin produced the most perfect sound ever heard. The boy picked up the violin and the bow and headed back to his caravan. And that was how the Gypsies discovered music.

I got a postcard of a tuna flying in the middle of a market in Seattle, Washington. Milan wrote: In Wales there lived a Gypsy they called Black Ellen. She was an expert storyteller. They say that she could spend all night telling just one story. They say that out of the blue, just to test her audience, Black Ellen would suddenly stop in the middle of a story and shout tshiocha, which means boots in Romany, and if her audience did not shout back cholova, which means socks in

Romany, Black Ellen would get up off the floor, shake out her skirt, and leave without finishing the story.

Sounds like Scheherazade, said Lía, in bra and panties and painting her toenails cherry red.

I got a postcard from Cleveland. It was a black-and-white portrait of a guitarist, seated, cigarette in mouth, sporting a thin mustache like Humphrey Bogart, or actually more like Fred Astaire. Milan wrote: Django Reinhardt was born in Belgium, though he just as easily could have been born in any country his Manouche Gypsy caravan was passing through. His father was a musician and his mother was a singer. As a boy, Django displayed the following talents: stealing chickens; finding and cleaning World War I bullet cartridges, whose casings his mother then reworked and sold as jewelry and brass finger cymbals; catching river trout just by thrusting his bare hand into the water and tickling them with his fingers until, contented and spellbound, they simply let themselves be grabbed; and finally, of course, the guitar. At the age of twelve, with his family living in a Gypsy camp just outside of Paris, Django was already playing guitar at every bal-musette in the city. At the age of eighteen, after a fire his wife, Bella, had started accidentally, he was left with a deformed left hand, almost a hook, yet somehow he managed to change his technique (using only two fingers now) and continued to play, eventually becoming the greatest jazz guitarist in the world. And yet always, when it came down to it, a Gypsy guitarist. Andrés Segovia heard him play once and was so impressed that he asked to see the score, but Django just laughed and told him that there wasn't one, that it was a simple improvisation. Jean Cocteau said of Django: He lived as one dreams of living, in a caravan, and even when it was no longer a caravan, somehow it still was. Although his legal name was Jean Reinhardt, he'd been called Django since he was a boy. Django, in Romany, means awake, or more precisely, I awaken. It's a first-person verb. I awaken.

I got a postcard of the Golden Gate Bridge, sent from San Francisco. Milan wrote: Last night, as I was playing in a beautiful auditorium, everything began to tremble. Some people stood. Others left. And I kept playing Stravinsky as if nothing much were happening. Nothing much was happening. In Romany, Eduardito, earthquake is I phuv kheldias, which means the earth danced.

I got two giant postcards, on the same day, from Orlando. Liszt I, the first was titled, and it was a picture of Donald Duck dressed as a fireman. Milan wrote: You asked me that night, in that strange cafeteria in Antigua, why I felt such an attraction to Liszt's music. Remember? And I replied with some nonsense about improvisation, which I suppose is true. But there's always more than one truth to everything. And a movie was made based on that other truth, a very complicated truth that is the life and music of Franz Liszt. I can't recall the name of the movie and it's not even very good, but it illustrates the point I want to make. I hope you understand. It's the year 1840, or thereabouts. Franz Liszt and Count Teleky arrive at a Gypsy carnival in Pest,

Hungary. As they saunter through the town square, Liszt is talking to his friend about the difference between a mere performer and a true composer. Suddenly, Liszt's attention is captured by a Gypsy boy playing the violin with such virtuosity that he immediately reminds him of Paganini. Josy, the boy's name is, and he says he'll do a magic trick if they give him some spare change. Count Teleky gives him some coins and the boy disappears, running off. They set out down the town's narrow streets to look for him but only find his older brother and grandmother, a very shrewd and very kind old lady who, after a brief debate, ends up reading Liszt's future. I can't recall what she says, but he, frightened, slips into the crowd. That night, Liszt is sitting there at his piano, trying to recall the melody Josy played. He can't. He gets mad, goes out to look for him, and finally finds him at the Gypsy camp, playing the violin once more. Liszt attempts to convince the boy's family that talent like his needs instruction and tutelage and refinement and culture, but Josy loves his freedom too much and won't accept the offer. Liszt insists. He wants to save him from savagery. He wants to Europeanize him. When the grandmother finds out that the man will not only teach him free of charge but also cover his room and board, she agrees, on the condition that she accompany her grandson. Later, all three pull up to Liszt's residence in a carriage. The servants wash and dress Josy, but the boy eats with his hands, runs wild, scribbles all over a bust of Beethoven. Meanwhile, Count Teleky bets Liszt that he won't be able to train the Gypsy boy in time for the annual music competition. Josy is wary of musical scores, believes in improvisation, refuses to learn music theory, and keeps playing by ear. Liszt begins to grow desperate. With a bit of help from the grandmother, Josy agrees at least to try this new way of playing music, and he and Liszt start playing together. And they both like it. They have a good time. One night, Josy hears his teacher give a recital and is enthralled. After the recital, at some type of dinner or formal reception, I don't really remember, Josy agrees to play a piece for the guests. But suddenly a woman screams that someone's stolen her gold bracelet, and everyone suspects the Gypsy. Humiliated, Josy runs away. The bracelet, of course, turns out to have fallen between some cushions or onto a rug or something. On returning home that night, Liszt finds Josy in the bathtub, scrubbing and scraping himself raw with a bar of soap. He wants, he says, sobbing, to wash off his Gypsy color. Every time I see this scene it makes me want to vomit.

Lía glanced at the postcard, said Goofy had always been her favorite, and then asked me sweetly, as if it was nothing, if Franz Liszt hadn't been an anti-Semite.

The second postcard from Orlando was titled Liszt II. It was another Donald Duck drawing, but this duck was dressed as a painter or a bricklayer, maybe—it wasn't too clear. Milan wrote: The day of the competition arrives. Josy is ready. When it's finally his turn, he begins to play beautifully, a virtuoso, a child prodigy, but then suddenly, for no apparent reason, he begins to improvise. The judges disqualify him. Josy is furious and disappointed and runs off. Back at home, Liszt sits before the piano and, still moved by the Gypsy boy's music, composes a piece, one of his Hungarian Rhapsodies, I think, without realizing the influence Josy's music has had on him. Count Teleky points this out, but Liszt resents the idea that he might have needed any

Gypsy influences to finally become a true composer. Liszt accepts that he has lost the bet. Josy leaps into the room. He'd been spying on them through the window, from the garden. He accuses Liszt of using him just to win a bet, and no matter how Liszt tries to make him see that he has a magical ability to capture the true spirit of music, Josy says they come from two different worlds that will never meet. The movie, in my opinion, should have ended there. Though perhaps not. I don't know. At any rate, Liszt rushes off to the Gypsy camp and returns with all of Josy's family and friends. He wants the boy to play his own music, with his own people, for Liszt's guests. Josy is upstairs. He refuses to come down. Slowly, the Gypsy music begins. Everyone shouts and sings and dances. Josy can't deny his true character and descends the stairs, picks his old violin up off the floor, and joins in the Gypsy revelry. Everyone applauds. Bravo. Liszt has accepted the Gypsies and has also accepted the spirit of Gypsy music and everyone's happy and the world is fucking peachy and that's the end. Do you understand?

I got a postcard that should have arrived much earlier, lost for a time in the hidden recesses of Milan's subconscious or perhaps in the hidden recesses of the post office's labyrinthine inefficiency, or both. The postmark said Savannah, Georgia. It was a sepia-colored photo of two elderly black men, solemn and looking preserved in a sweltering vat of muggy air. They were on the porch of a stately old southern home, relaxing in wooden and wicker rocking chairs and sipping lemonade or perhaps iced tea. Also on the porch were a brown cat and a porcelain pot, probably a spittoon. One of the old men had a peg leg. Milan wrote: Ciganin, that's what they called me at school. It means Gypsy, in Serbian. Ciganin. Or sometimes Cigo. Cigo, and then they'd call me names or throw rocks at me or give me a kick in the ass. To Serbs I've always been a piece of shit Gypsy, a filthy good-for-nothing Gypsy. And to Gypsies I've always been a piece of shit gadje, a piece of shit non-Gypsy. My mother's family rejected us. My father's family rejected us. I'm a Gypsy who can't be a Gypsy and a Serb who can't be a Serb. What's a boy to do, Eduardito, when he's excluded by one group and excluded by the other and detested by both? He withdraws, that's what he does. He retreats into himself. And that, no doubt, is my greatest talent. Not music, but the ability to close myself off, ignore people and, what's more, get people to ignore me. It's not that I become invisible, as invisibility still implies presence, observation, being a witness, even if a distant, disinterested witness. I can absent myself entirely. Eliminate myself entirely. Not like a corpse, but more like someone who never existed. A world without me.

Maybe because of the photo of the two elderly black men, maybe because of the confessional tone Milan used, this was Lía's favorite postcard. She would come into my studio and, lighting the obligatory cigarette, contemplate it for a long time as though contemplating something sacred, something mysterious, something that was in fact something else or at least seemed to be something else.

Gyorgy, read the title on the next postcard, a very large postcard of the London Underground logo. In minuscule

letters, Milan wrote: Last year the body of a Gypsy trumpeter named Gyorgy Krompachy turned up floating in the
Copşa Mică River, in Romania. No one knows why. I'd met
him at a weeklong Gypsy music festival in Lucerne. Even
though he was my age, he looked much older. He smoked a
mixture of hash and tobacco and drank vodka from a rusty
canteen. He said vodka was good for playing in seven-eight
time, whiskey was good for playing in six-eight, absinthe for
playing in nine-eight. I think he was right. Though he was
born in Bulgaria, he didn't consider himself Bulgarian. He'd
hop around from Serbian bands to Macedonian bands to
Romanian bands to Turkish bands without thinking twice,
as if they were modern versions of kumpanias or the caravans of his ancestors. But what he liked to play best, he said,
were Serbian kolos, very fast circular dances that were really intense and made him feel, he said, as though he had
a very high fever. Similar to Jewish dances. With overstated
pride, Gyorgy told me he'd made a brief appearance in the
bunker scenes of the Emir Kusturica movie *Underground* "(I
thought of him, Eduardito, when I bought this postcard a
few weeks ago). I didn't believe him, of course, though a long
while later I discovered it was true. There he was, Gyorgy
Krompachy, smiling and composed and playing his trumpet
on top of the spinning cake when the bride goes flying over
them. The last night of the festival, after playing a couple of
čočeks with Kočani Orkestar, a band from Macedonia, Gyorgy asked me to accompany him to the outskirts of town,
on an errand. He was dressed in black, with a sparkling green
vest and sparkling white shoes. First, we went to a bar, where
Gyorgy had one vodka, and then another vodka, and then,
in exchange for a few bills, pawned his trumpet. I remember

that before he handed it over, he showed me the inside of its black case, papered over with naked ladies, all Asian. After that, we went to a little shack of mud and corrugated metal, in the middle of nowhere. A Gypsy woman, maybe forty or fifty years old, opened the door. She had gold teeth. Smelled bad. Gyorgy gave her the money and the woman, smiling maliciously, closed the door. That was it. We walked back to the festival tents, with Gyorgy smoking his tobacco and hash and going on and on about Thai vaginas and how enormous they are. The next day, when I woke up he'd already left.

I got a postcard of the streets of New York City. In Central Park, a couple of perfect models with perfect tans skated into a perfect sunset. Milan wrote: Some time ago, Félix Lajkó, the most famous Gypsy violinist from Novi Sad, was passing through town. He played in Madison Square Garden. After the concert, several of the Serbian artists living in Manhattan decided to take him out to dinner. Writers, painters, a filmmaker. I didn't say a word the whole night. I spent two hours sitting next to one of my idols, in the most absolute silence, petrified. When the coffee was finally served, Lajko turned to me and said that he knew an accordionist whose last name was Rakić who was also from Belgrade, and maybe he was family. Without looking up from my espresso, I whispered that no relative of mine was an accordionist in Belgrade. And that was it.

I got a postcard of a cowboy on horseback, from San Antonio, Texas. Milan wrote: Long, long ago, the Gypsies built a church of stone and the Serbs built a church of cheese. When each of the churches was finished, they decided to swap. The Gypsies would give the Serbs the church of stone, and the Serbs would give the Gypsies the church of cheese, plus five cents. But as the Serbs had no money, they still owed the Gypsies the five cents. Immediately the Gypsies began to eat their church of cheese, and little by little they polished it off. And then they had no church. The Serbs still owe the Gypsies five cents, and the Gypsies still demand it every day. I think the time has come, Eduardito, to settle that five-cent debt with myself. Tshiocha, I cry, like that beautiful black Welsh woman.

There then followed a long silence. As if the angst had overwhelmed him and so, wishing me the best, he'd dived headfirst into the earth's core. Initially, I thought perhaps something had gone wrong at the post office, some technical failure or some kind of epistolary disruption, but I quickly discarded that theory, given all the bills and junk mail I kept receiving. Then I thought something had happened to Milan. An illness, or something worse. His postcards had been so punctual, one a week, sometimes two or three a week, and I'd gotten hooked on them almost without realizing it, the way you might get hooked on sleeping pills or a bad soap opera or a six o'clock Cinzano with lots of ice. Lía made fun of me, look how worried you are, Dudú, watching me arrange and then rearrange and then disarrange all of the postcards on my studio wall: first chronologically, then geographically, then thematically, then photographically. I was worried, no doubt, but I also understood, even if only hypothetically, that part of Milan's game consisted of straying from the path, absenting himself, disappearing for a time and leaving no trace, no signs of any sort. It was one more way of breaching boundaries and borders: the boundaries and borders of a routine or of a preestablished, systematic path. It was, I suspect, one more way of always playing the least predictable piece.

Making the most of two weeks we had off from the university—Lía from her last few anatomy courses, and I from giving a yearlong series of seminars on screenplays adapted from short stories—I packed all of my recently acquired Gypsy music and, for seven days, we escaped to a frozen, secluded cabin in a village called Albores, in the Sierra de las Minas: a biosphere reserve in the cloud forest, almost three thousand meters above sea level.

We spent the days looking for venomous snakes (pit vipers and rattlers, mostly), noisy howler monkeys, owls, wild turkeys, pink-headed warblers, and, astonishingly, a flock of shimmering red-and-green quetzals perched on the branches of immense wild avocado trees, and which later took off with the synchronized, rhythmic undulations of a paper kite. We regularly came across peccaries' tracks in the mud and, from time to time, those of a big cat. Jaguars, the park ranger told us with hazy affability. Each morning, over our first coffee, a mob of blue magpies breakfasted with us on the balcony, pecking our crumbs off the floor and the table and sometimes even out of our hands.

We spent the nights making love (there's nothing like making love in a biosphere reserve) and listening to the violin and magic sitar of Félix Lajkó; the Hungarian café music called olah, by Kek Lang and Kalyi Jag; the robust songs of Rajasthan; Darko Macura's duduk; Turkish clarinets; Egyptian drums; Kálmán Balogh's cimbalom; the brash, fast trumpets of Boban Marković and Jova Stojilković; the unstoppable guitars of French Manouche Gypsies; the voice of Macedonian singer Esma Redžepova; and a lot of flamenco. The music played and we made love in an almost primitive manner, an almost prehistoric manner, as if all of the cries and the drums and the pain and the moon and the clouds and the shrieking of all those bats were also there with us, between the sheets.

Lía, like a doctor, or perhaps more like a scientist, or perhaps more like a zealous disciple of quantum physics, ended up associating various types of Gypsy music with different positions. Automatically. Without realizing it, of course. I began to infer certain patterns on the third or fourth night, but they remained unconfirmed until the fifth. Kolos: her on top. Sambas: me on top. Olahs: both seated, facing one another, legs entwined. Flamenco: her on top, both faceup. Rumbas: both on our sides, facing each other. Čočeks: me on top, her facedown. Ciftetelis: the position she called zero gravity because that's apparently what she felt, zero gravity, but which I find nearly impossible to describe. The music would change and Lía, just as quickly, would turn me over or push me down or jump on top of me with the uninhibited agility of a young gazelle. And the more drumming, needless to say, the more noise she made. On our last night, I explained this all to her and Lía laughed and said you're crazy, Dudú, and made me turn off the music before I could take off her clothes.

Perhaps it was that music, perhaps it was the mountain altitude and the cold, or perhaps it was the fact that we were so alone and when two people are so alone their spirits seek to express themselves even more exquisitely, but even Lía's orgasms were transformed. Seven sketches made by someone else, drawn by another hand. Seven pages of her almond-colored notebook that bore no relation to any of the pages that had come before and that would bear no relation to any of the pages that were to come. A seven-orgasm parenthesis, one might say, though I'm not entirely convinced by that stylistic device. The lines were now more curved than straight, much more tenuous and unsure, as though they'd been drawn when frightened or perhaps when sleepy. The blank spaces took on greater importance, giving the sketches a desert-like air or a flighty air, where the emptiness seemed exclusively to be filled with more empti-ness and where silence was the only thing you could hear and the only thing really worth hearing. The different signs and symbols also underwent a profound metamorphosis: streams and clouds and craters and spasms were still there, but nearly unrecognizable. On that last night, the seventh, with only the music of all the bats twittering in the grooves of the ceiling, Lía sat on the edge of the bed, turned on a small lamp, and covered in goose bumps from the cold or perhaps from something more esoteric, closed that brief parenthesis with a quick sketch of a spiderweb being spun.

We returned to the city exhausted. The pinkish sun was setting slowly, like the fake backdrop to an indulgent final scene. We showered together and then Lía made us two cups of coffee. Lazily, stretched out across my bed, we smoked a couple of cigarettes and played footsie and perhaps we dozed off. I don't know why I waited so long to check my mailbox. Probably because it was Sunday. Probably because, deep down, I already knew what was awaiting me and, even deeper down, I also knew what I'd inevitably have to do.

One postcard.

From above, the Danube looked like a dead earthworm, or maybe like a dying earthworm, amid so much gray debris. A vast white bridge intersected it like a fishhook. Little houses dotted one shore, and on the other, surrounded by a considerable patch of green, stood some sort of citadel or fortress or medieval castle. Kalemegdan, it said on the lower right of the photo. Srbija, read the postmark unequivocally.

Once upon a time, dear Eduardito, there was a half-Serbian and half-Gypsy boy who wanted to be a Gypsy musician and travel in a Gypsy musician caravan, but something held him back. Perhaps fear. Perhaps something else. As he was walking one morning through the damp forests of Belgrade, there suddenly appeared before him a very large man with purple eyes, dressed in red, with two little horns on his head and a hoof for one of his feet, and he told the boy, as he stroked him with a long, sharp fingernail, that he could turn him into a Gypsy musician, a great Gypsy musician, on one condition. Just one. There's always a condition, right, Eduardito? Always a sacrifice. That's the law of the universe. So the boy, happy and sad, said goodbye to his father forever and said goodbye to his mother forever, and weeping in the forests of Belgrade which were now to become his home, he performed a single pirouette.

Ghosts

Why do you want to find him, Dudú?

I was nearly finished packing my suitcase, and Lía, in her sky blue doctor's outfit, was still lying on her back on the floor, riffling through all the postcards.

I didn't say anything. I didn't have an answer. I still don't. I still don't know why I wanted to find Milan Rakić. Nor am I altogether sure when or how I decided to travel to Belgrade.

Perhaps the idea began to germinate in my mind because of all those postcards, through all those stories that I somehow began to think of as my own. And perhaps it continued to incubate during the whole year I hadn't received any news at all from Milan. And perhaps it ended up taking its obsession-like shape when I came across the perfect little bow for my Balkan parcel by the name of Danica Kovasević, a very beautiful, very Serbian girl who had been living in Guatemala for more than a decade.

I met her at a trendy nightclub. Before introducing me to her, a friend whispered to me that although she claimed to work as a publicist, she was actually a very high-class prostitute. One of those really top-end ones, compadre, he said with a smell of artificial tequila on his breath, staring out at some distant mountaintop kingdom. That night, in the midst of all the commotion and the noise of some kind of electronic music, I told Danica (stressed on the middle syllable, not the first, she said, correcting me) that I wanted to travel to Belgrade, though it's also quite likely that after two or three whiskies I actually told her that I needed to travel to Belgrade, since whiskey, as we all know, as my Polish grandfather knew particularly well, tends to sharpen the notes of necessity. She smiled and said oh, right, evidently skeptical. But the following day, I phoned her and told her again that I wanted to take advantage of an invitation to Póvoa de Varzim, in Portugal, to travel to Belgrade and that I also wanted her help in getting my bearings and perhaps finding somewhere to stay. I've even bought my plane ticket, I told her, lying. Danica said to give her a couple of days, that she'd call me back. She called two weeks later. All set, she said. A friend of mine, Slavko Nikolić, will pick you up at the airport, and he'll take you himself to an apartment on Nedeljka Cabrinovića, and I immediately pictured a dirty, dark little room used as a base for underage whores and human trafficking. I said nothing, just weighing up my stupidity. It's very cheap, she said, don't worry. Slavko's a good guy, she added. In the background I heard a rough male voice saying something or asking for something, and Danica hung up without saying goodbye. Giving plenty of notice, then, I informed the university that I was going to be taking two weeks' vacation, accepted the invitation to Portugal entirely as a pretext (I wrote my "Speech at Póvoa" a few days prior to leaving, after an endless night of Bergman and insomnia), and without giving any of it too much thought I bought myself a complicated plane ticket that included a stay in Belgrade. Simple as that. Irrational as that.

But I nearly didn't go. Ten days before the trip, I got in touch with the Serbian embassy in Mexico (there isn't one in Guatemala) in order to obtain a tourist visa. Right away, they sent me a checklist of requirements, a pretty ridiculous and pretty long checklist that included, besides photocopies of bank statements and a record of my credit history, a letter from the person in Belgrade who was inviting me, signed and authenticated by a notary. We need the original letter, a girl from the embassy told me over the phone. Sorry, no scans, do you understand? she insisted in a thick accent and a paranoid tone of voice, but I thought I'd heard her say: Sorry, no can do, you understand? I immediately called Danica and she said to send Slavko Nikolić an e-mail explaining the situation. A few days later, he replied in ratlike Spanish to say he was sorry but that it would be impossible to procure the letter—that was the word he used, procure—and I imagined an endless line of Serbs trying to get their hands on a bit of hard bread and tinned sardines and, with any luck, a roll of toilet paper. He said that he was very sorry, but the previous week he'd slipped on a patch of ice and was now in bed with a broken leg. Just about ready to toss my ticket in the trash (in a manner of speaking), I sent another e-mail to the embassy in Mexico, explaining the situation to them, and the following day they replied that I needn't worry about the letter, that it wasn't a problem, that they'd make an exception in my case. That they'd what? An exception? Sometime later, I learned that the Serbian ambassador in

Mexico was Mrs. Vesna Pesić, who had been a political ac-
tivist at the time of the fall of Milošević, and was the wife
of an American economist who, mysteriously, fortuitously,
was also a professor and a colleague of mine from the university in Guatemala. I never found out for sure whether
that had anything to do with the sudden and merciful
waiving of the visa, but three days before leaving I already
had my passport back with a firmly stuck-on Serbian decal,
which said, in ancient-looking typed letters, Turisticki.

Why do you want to find him, Dudú? Lía had asked me
again, now out of her little doctor's outfit, while she was
putting all the postcards—along with the photo of a very
serious-looking Milan Rakić that we'd cut out of a Guatemalan newspaper—into an old yellow envelope.

I never answered her. I don't know whether one single
answer existed. I don't think so. There's always more than
one truth to everything, Milan had written in one of his
postcards. The why of an action is a kind of intellectual
crossword, it occurred to me then or it occurs to me now,
in which you try to fill in the little empty boxes that get
tangled up with one another, that mix and lean into one
another, in which no one answer is worth more or less than
any other and also where each answer might on its own
seem irrational or even downright crazy. But when they
are brought together, they complement and strengthen one
another. Or something like that. I felt seduced, I guess,
seduced by his music, seduced by his postcards, seduced
by his story, seduced by the revolutionary tremors of his
spirit, seduced by a smoky, erotic image that I wouldn't be
able to make out clearly until the very end of my stay in
Belgrade. And a man seduced doesn't measure anything the

same way, not time, not the force of gravity, and especially not distances. The only thing I understood, really understood, was that I was obsessed with the idea of looking for him, that I needed to look for him perhaps in the same way that a curious, morbid, slightly fearful child needs to look under the bed for ghosts.

The Pirouette

Like I was drugged right there in Barajas airport, like I was floating in a dream dreamed by someone else who was surprised to see me but also found it pitiable and let me just carry on floating, I took a Swissair flight from Madrid to Belgrade.

I prefer a window seat, but I got the aisle. Two kids of about nine or ten sat down next to me. Little brothers expatriated during the war, I thought, now going back to visit their uncles and cousins and grandparents. Both of them were nervous. I tried to say something to them in French, but I don't think they understood me at all; I just made them more nervous. On the other side of me, across the aisle, a beautiful girl of about seventeen sat down. Slim and blond, her fingernails painted scarlet, she wore huge dark glasses with white plastic frames that looked like they were left over from the seventies. She took off her shoes and socks. Her feet were dirty. Suddenly, one of the kids next to me started crying and his brother scuttled off to tell the flight attendant. I tried to offer him a stick of gum, but he just hugged tighter his purple elephant. He told the flight attendant he had a stomachache and the flight attendant brought him a room-temperature Coke. His little brother knelt on the floor and, using the seat as a table, started drawing soccer players in a huge notebook. The blond girl said something to me in Serbian or maybe Russian—I don't know—that sounded like the swishing of a bunch of magnolias, which is, of course, pretty implausible, given I've never heard the swishing of a bunch of magnolias. I smiled the forced smile of an idiot.

I could have sworn the immigration officer at Belgrade airport was a character out of a Tarkovsky film. Maybe Andrei Rublev himself. He sat there smoking sternly and looking at me as if the night before I'd fucked his virgin daughter. I said I was sorry, just in case, and put my passport through the gap in the thick bulletproof glass, and without looking up he started to bend it, scratch it, tug at it, rub the laminated pages with his greasy thumb. Another officer was standing just behind him, watching the whole thing over his shoulder. The officer in the seat showed my passport to his friend, who grabbed it and bent it and scratched it and then went off somewhere with it. Maybe to some other supervisor who was watching it all from an even greater height, so that he could scratch it too. An ominous and infinite pyramid of Serbian scratchers, I thought. The first officer stayed in his seat, smoking. In English, his eyes fixed on my mouth, he asked me why I'd come to Belgrade, and for how long, and could he see my return ticket, and how much money did I have with me, and also was I carrying any plastic (that threw me, maybe because I was nervous, until he said credit card), and where would I be staying, and where was my letter of invitation. My what? Your letter, he repeated through the bulletproof glass, his cigarette clouding everything with smoke. My knees grew weak and I felt a gust of cool air in my stomach and I was convinced that in the airport of the former Yugoslavian capital you could clearly feel the earth's rotation. My what? Letter, he shouted at me for the third time. But Vesna Pesić, the ambassador to Mexico, I stuttered, like a frightened little rabbit. I regretted it. The guy frowned and looked even sterner and in my mind I saw him pulling his stone-age revolver on me at any minute, then I imagined a small room, my body tied to a chair, the injection to make me tell them all my truths. The other officer came back with my passport and said something to his colleague in the chair. They both laughed. I felt a faint urge to cry. The officer stubbed his cigarette out in an ashtray already full of butts, and without a word he handed my passport and money and credit cards back through the gap in the bulletproof glass.

I came out of the airport, and I don't know why—since Slavko Nikolić had told me about it in his last e-mail—but I was surprised to see everything covered in white. I was overcome by a deep sense of peace, of well-being, of harmony, a feeling that snow only arouses in people who live in the tropics. I opened my backpack for my hat and scarf. It was getting dark.

Just then, a pale woman with straw-colored hair said my name. I'm Zdena Lecić, Slavko's girlfriend, she said in English, and held out her hand with a charming smile. And this is my father, Marko Lecić, as she indicated a short and stooped and cheerful man who immediately made me think of Bela Lugosi at the end of his life, or rather of a very cadaverous Martin Landau playing Bela Lugosi at the end of his life. I'm the driver, he said with a smoker's voice and in an appalling English accent, and between chuckles and nasty coughs he clapped me hard on the back.

We got into a red Yugo that looked like it was about to collapse but that still worked pretty well, notwithstanding any tempting Yugoslav allegories. From the backseat, Zdena told me we'd go to her house first so we could all have dinner with Slavko, and that later her dad would take me to the apartment. The chauffeur, joked Marko, raising his hand. I was exhausted by the journey, but what could I do? Zdena explained to me that since her boyfriend had broken his leg, he'd decided to move in with them, as her dad's house was a lot more spacious. It's better for everyone, she added. I asked what Slavko did for a living, but they both stayed oddly quiet. Marko said something in Serbian and then said in English that before we did anything else we'd have to stop in at the police station. I thought he was joking. You have to register, he said seriously. Zdena laughed. How do you mean, register? All tourists have to register with the police when they arrive in the country, said Marko as we crossed a vast white bridge that reminded me of Milan's last postcard. And all tourists have to register again before they leave the country, he added. Check in and check out, like in a hotel, I thought, but I didn't say anything. We passed by one bombed-out building, then another, and another. I asked why they left them like that, why they didn't knock them down. Supposedly, said Zdena, there are unexploded bombs inside. And there's no money for it, said Marko as he parked the Yugo next to a pink building, a real bubblegum pink, a tutti-frutti pink: the only pink building in an utterly gray city. Is this the police station? I asked doubtfully. There was no sign outside. You need to show them your passport and plane ticket, Marko told me as he opened his door. I'll wait for you guys here, said Zdena, still smiling. And so, documents in hand, I started walking toward the pink building, and it occurred to me, rather melodramatically, that the whole thing reeked of a goddamn ambush.

The inside of the police station was dirty and crumbling. It stank. Just like a Latin American police station, I thought. Marko asked a policeman something and the policeman pointed to a door at the end of a long corridor. Savski Venac, said the little label on the door. Suspicious, I asked Marko what it meant and he replied that it was the name of that area of the city. We went in. A policeman with a sour face got up and immediately, instinctively, put his hand on the revolver in his belt. Marko explained everything to him. The policeman took my documents. We have to wait outside, whispered Marko, and we went back out into the corridor. When we were sitting down, he told me not to worry, that everyone from the old regime was high-strung and grumpy. They still believe in intimidation, he added. A woman in pearls and an ostentatious white fur coat was also waiting outside. She looked downcast. She looked worn-out. I noticed that her makeup had run, as though she'd been crying or sweating or something. And I felt like I was in a Tarkovsky film again. Or even better: in a Fellini film—not the Fellini of tangos and flaming tridents, but the Fellini of every man for himself, gentlemen, galloping off on a sea horse. After a while, the same policeman came out, gave me back my documents, and off we went.

The Lecić house—a welcoming little homestead of clay and tiles built at the beginning of the last century—was on Puškinova Street, in an area of Belgrade known as Topčidersko Brdo. The apartment where they were going to put me up, Zdena told me as we got out the car, was very close by, just ten minutes away by taxi, in a neighborhood called Banovo Brdo.

That's my dad's studio, explained Zdena, pointing to a small building to one side of the house. We're both painters, she said. Through the studio window, a few dogs started barking unenthusiastically, out of pure habit.

Slavko Nikolić was lying back on a sofa, his leg in plaster, a pack of Lucky Strikes in his hand. He was a big guy, maybe six six, with long, disheveled dark hair and a face that I thought was halfway between conceited and affectionate, like a piping hot rice pudding without enough cinnamon.

Sorry I couldn't come and pick you up at the airport, Eduardo, he said in very broken Spanish, holding out his hand (a cyclops's hand) and with a curious accent that was part Serbian and part Catalan. I told him this. Yeah, I lived in Barcelona nearly three years. In the Barrio Gótico. That's where I learned Spanish. During the bombings. Sit down, sit down. Marko asked him for a cigarette and then, in English, said he'd go and see how dinner was doing. Slavko poured two small glasses of a light coffee-colored liqueur. It's called Stomaklija, he said. Welcome, he said. Živeli, he said, and we downed it in one gulp. It tasted a bit like a mature rum, but not as sweet and with some sort of herb added. Rosemary, perhaps. I took a cigarette out of his pack. You a friend of Danica's, then? he asked me, pronouncing Danica in such an odd way (all the syllables

at once) that it took me a while to reply that yes, well, I
didn't know about friends, since I'd only met her recently.
Unusually nervous, I asked him what he did for a living,
but Slavko just gave a slightly patronizing, mawkish smile.
She's a good girl, Danica, he said, and then he was quiet.
We smoked for a while in silence. This is for you, I said, and
I handed him an envelope of money for the rent. Taking it,
Slavko suddenly started lamenting the country's economic
situation, and the country's political situation. Making
a huge effort, I managed to follow for a minute or two,
and then, as always happens when someone launches into
some speech about politics and politicians and politicking,
I started thinking about naked women. I don't know why.
Maybe just out of habit, maybe to keep myself occupied,
maybe because I associate acts of power with sexual acts,
maybe it's got something to do with being Jewish.

For dinner we had a salad with tomato and cucumber and spicy paprika, then something called gibanica,
which was like filo pastry with spinach and cheese. While
we ate, Slavko carried on pouring me shots of the light
coffee-colored liqueur and Marko talked to me about his
grandfather or maybe his great-grandfather who was one
of the most famous painters in the country. I wanted to
ask him what country, as the geographical situation still
had me pretty confused, but I decided it was inopportune,
and besides, I wasn't in the mood for more conversations
about politics. Yugoslavia, I whispered, half-drunk now,
but I don't think anyone heard or maybe they did. Marko
said that afterward he'd show me a book with some of the
famous painter's works. Hvala, thanks, I said, and everyone laughed. Slavko got out another bottle and, pouring

me out some transparent liqueur, said try it, try it, it's
called viljamovka. It tasted of pear. And without asking,
he poured me another. Zdena had prepared a pot of coffee,
four cups exactly, and we all started to smoke and drink
coffee in silence. A delicious silence. Marko suddenly
belched, loudly and without the slightest bit of embarrassment, and as though that were some sort of signal, I told
them that I loved Gypsy music, that I loved the music of
Serbian Gypsies, and wondered where I could hear some
live. Well, on the streets, said Marko, that lot are always
going round begging and playing trumpets and violins.
And no one said anything else.

I hugged Slavko goodbye and then Zdena and her dad
took me to the little apartment on Nedeljka Čabrinovića.
Marko waited in the car. Even though I was a bit drunk, I
managed to make it up the four flights of stairs and listen
to Zdena as she explained how to open the door and how
to turn on the water heater. It's Slavko's apartment, she
said, but we've fixed it up a bit for you. I thanked her. Seriously, Zdena, I'm really interested in Gypsy music, I said
with a mixture of pathos and pleading that took me right
back to being seven years old, standing at the gates of the
zoo, and what a tantrum I threw with my mother because
I was so bent on her buying me a wrestling mask, the one
that El Santo wore. Zdena just smiled. Then she wrote the
addresses and phone numbers on a slip of paper and told
me that I should take only taxis marked Beo or Yellow or
Pink or Lux or Maxis or Bell and no others. Do viđenja,
she said, which means goodbye. Do viđenja, I repeated.

I went to bed without getting undressed and without

unpacking anything, and I remember that the last thing I thought of before falling into a deep sleep was the word Yugoslavia.

I woke up with a headache, but two aspirins and a long, hot shower made me feel much better. I was about to go out, when the phone rang. It was Zdena. In a sleepy voice, she told me she'd been thinking about what I'd asked her about Gypsy music and that I could walk down Knez Mihajlova Street, or through a bohemian neighborhood called Skadarlija. Write it down. Skadarlija. There are some really nice cafés there where Gypsies play sometimes. I thanked her, and in the background I could hear Slavko whispering something. Listen, Slavko says that he's going to be here all day, working, so you can come over whenever you like. Working on what? I thought a bit apprehensively, but I just thanked her again. Before I hung up, Zdena listed the names of the genuine taxi companies again, one by one.

It was snowing softly. I was hungry and wanted a coffee, but I didn't have any local currency with me. Dinars, they're called. After walking down Pozeska Street for a while, I went into a bank, and a woman who I thought looked like a chubby, Balkan version of Penelope Cruz, although I'm not sure why—her mouth, perhaps—asked me to show her my passport and fill out some forms. I had to wait almost half an hour before she gave me a wad of old bills that, oddly, still said Banka Jugoslavije. What a mess of a country, I thought as I walked out. Next to the bank there was a little café. It was empty. On one wall they'd hung two photos: one of Tito and one, a little bigger, of the

CHiPs cops, the dark one and the blond one, holding their helmets. Coffee, I said to the waiter, miming a huge cup of coffee. Kafa, he said, and then he said something else. I just shrugged. I pointed to some ham rolls that he had on the counter and that looked a bit stale. I finished everything quickly, gave him a few dinars, almost nothing really, and walked out. It wasn't snowing anymore but it wasn't sunny either. At a kiosk I bought a pack of Lucky Strikes (Slavko's influence, of course), a lighter, and two bars of chocolate, and then, already on my way to the bohemian quarter that Zdena had made me write the name of, I felt slightly nervous as I realized I hadn't checked the name of the taxi company. I opened the window, lit a cigarette, and put on my best murderer's face.

People wrapped up in gray and black. More bombed-out buildings. New smells and sounds that were also somehow the same ones as always. There's nothing like the fear of getting lost in an unknown city, I thought as I saw the guy's shrewd eyes in the rearview mirror. We went past the pink police station, and for some reason I felt safer. We stopped at a light. Some way off, sitting alone on what seemed to be a Persian rug, was a kid dressed in rags, playing the accordion. Ciganin? I asked the taxi driver—I don't know how I remembered the word—and he nodded. He said something that sounded like an insult. I gave him a bit of money and got out.

The kid was dressed up, even though everything clashed with everything else: olive green jacket, corduroy pants, green-and-blue-striped shirt, gray felt hat. I threw a coin into the little bronze pot he had by his shoes, and without stopping, he smiled with his half-rotten teeth. It was the same Gypsy music I already knew, but it was also completely different. More visceral, or maybe more rural. The tune sounded sweet and bitter at the same time. Like his face, I thought. Beneath the music, beyond the music, I could hear his little fingernails tip-tapping on the keys and buttons. I knelt down. He stopped without looking up. I threw another coin into the bronze pot and he started playing again. And we went back and forth like that for a while, like cat and mouse. Every time the music stopped, I'd throw another coin and he'd play for a bit before stopping again. At one of these moments, when the kid stopped playing, he told me something in Serbian or maybe in Romany. I just shrugged and shook my head, but the kid kept talking and laughing as if I understood him or as if it didn't matter if I understood him. Then, still talking to me, he started to play chords that somehow accompanied what he was telling me. Sometimes it sounded like a story, sometimes like a song, and sometimes it sounded like a joke. Impossible to know. He stopped playing. He asked me something and this time waited in silence for a reply. He stood up and asked me again, impatiently, almost annoyed. I got up too.

Then, out of nowhere, a Gypsy girl appeared, a bit older and a lot darker than he was, carrying a handful of withered roses. She wore a long, flowery dress, a flowery handkerchief on her head, and a thick, moth-eaten green wool sweater. She smelled like passion fruit. She handed me a rose and I gave her a ten-dinar bill. She took the bill and then picked up the coins from the bronze pot and put it all down her blouse, although she looked too young to be wearing a bra. I took out my cigarettes, and the boy, making a sign with his fingers, asked me for one. I held out the open pack.

He took five. She also took five. They both stashed their cigarettes away, took one more each, and put them in their mouths. I gave them a light. The girl grabbed my right hand and started tracing the lines of my palm with her index finger: she was reading it for me or acting as if she was reading it for me without my understanding anything. She looked delighted. Then she looked worried. She gave me back my hand and held out her own. I gave her another ten dinars. Then the boy, without taking his accordion off, rolled up the little rug, threw it over his shoulder, and the three of us started walking as we smoked.

It was like they existed outside of this world. I don't know how else to explain it. People mostly seemed to ignore them and, in turn, they mostly seemed to ignore people. They laughed, fooled around, and smoked happily away. They didn't bat an eyelid when a Serbian teenager spat on them. Nor when a man talking on his cell phone pushed past them. As though the two of them weren't even there. Negligible. Meaningless. Worse than immaterial. And watching them walk under an elegant dusting of snow that I decided was appropriate, I remembered Milan's greatest talent.

We walked a long way, I don't know how long, with me always three or four paces behind. They knew I was there, following them, but they didn't say anything to me, nor did they turn around to look at me except for when they felt like another cigarette. My pleasure, and we kept on walking in the same way.

It was getting dark. We entered a neighborhood that appeared more refined, less bombed-out, you could say, with restaurants and bars and little open-air cafés. The boy started playing a tune. The girl shouted something to me and grabbed my scarf and coiled it around her neck and started to twirl and dance as she skipped along, holding the withered roses out to passersby and shaking the bronze pot at them and singing who knows what words. They would make their way through the café terraces, circling around the densely packed tables, and the whole scene looked like it was taken from some Degas painting, only an aberrant and more proletarian one: Gypsy dancer instead of pompous ballerinas, Serbian workers instead of French intellectuals, and always, there in the background, an accordionist. Nobody paid them any attention, nobody gave them a penny, nobody wanted a rose, but they carried on just as lively and cheerful as before, and it occurred to me that singing and dancing mattered more to them than making money, and that money was just a pretext for singing and dancing and mocking everyone, because there's no doubt that, in their way, they were mocking everyone. I stayed a little way off, inspecting them like an embarrassed entomologist, but whether embarrassed for them or for the Serbs in general or for myself, I don't know.

They stopped in front of a food stall. An old mustachioed man started shouting something at them, waving his arms and shooing them away like you'd shoo away flies or stray dogs. I told him in English not to worry, that I'd pay. He seemed to understand. Still grumbling and complaining, he handed me three kebab sticks with some kind of meat on them. Ćevapčići, he said. The girl snatched them from me, and before I knew what was happening, the two of them had already disappeared around a corner with all the food. I sighed and forced a bitter, joyless smile, a wet socks kind of smile. The old man shook his head, as if to say I warned

you, you idiot. I asked him for another kebab and, still feeling a little mournful, ate it standing up, with a beer that was
too warm and then another beer that was also too warm. I
paid. I lit my last cigarette and walked off.

When I was already in who knows what kind of taxi, on
my way back to the apartment, it hit me that the little snake
had gone off with my scarf as well.

The next day, the phone woke me up. It was Slavko. He
said I should get ready quickly, that he and a friend would
come by in half an hour so we could go and get something
to drink, and he hung up.

Davor gets annoyed like a proper Montenegrin, said
Slavko in English, lying in the backseat, his leg stretched
right out. The great aesthetic of socialist architecture, said
Davor in the cumbersome English of a tour guide. That's
what he's like, he's reckless, added Slavko. Square gray building, square leaden building, and oh, what have we here,
said Davor with raised eyebrows and outstretched hand, a
square grayish building. So don't even think about annoy-
ing him, said Slavko. Please, Davor continued sternly, try
not to be quite so enthused about the brilliance of the ar-
chitects from socialist Yugoslavia. Then he said something
in Serbian and sighed. His name was Davor Zdravić. He
was tall, bearded, blond, already half-bald, and he worked
as a notary or a lawyer or something I didn't quite get. In
the sunken contours of his eyes was the naturally ironic,
gently caricatured air of one who smiles only when he is
being very serious. I like García Márquez, he said suddenly.
And also Cantinflas. Once, he said as he looked for a place

to park the car, I slept with a girl from Ecuador, which is almost like saying Guatemala, right?

Everything was still blanketed in snow. We walked to Akademski Plato. In the middle of the square was a pompous statue of a man. I walked up to it. Ngejoš, the plaque read. The poet Ngejoš, Slavko said to me, puffing out little curls of air vapor from the effort of walking on crutches. He was a governor of Montenegro, he said. He was a priest who wrote erotic poems. He may have died of syphilis.

We went into the Plato Kafe. A guy with a milky complexion and dressed in a black jacket and black tie greeted us from the back of the room. His tousled hair gave him a Bob Dylan sort of look, but Bob Dylan in those first photos, where he seems vulnerable, almost childishly annoyed at having been woken up so early. Slobodan Vrbanović, he said, holding out his hand and telling me in English that he worked for the newspaper *Danas*. A fifteen-year-old dressed in his father's suit, I thought, a suit from way back when that hung loosely over his pale and lanky body.

Slavko ordered four espressos and four vinjaks, which turned out to be a sort of cheap whiskey, and I ate a delicious pastry with cheese called kajmak. As Slavko and Davor began to bombard me with all the history and all the names and all the leaders that had paraded through this corner of the world, I tried not to think about naked women, and the boy reporter smoked in silence and bit his nails. Slavko: The word Balkan comes from the Turkish and means mountain. Davor: An important year, 1878, because for the first time, after centuries of Turkish rule from one side of the Danube and Austro-Hungarian rule from the other, Serbia, Montenegro, and Romania finally become independent. Slavko: And an autonomous Hungary is created. Davor: But all the others, meaning Croatia, Slovenia, and Bosnia-Herzegovina, remain under Austro-Hungarian control until the First World War. Davor again: And 1912's another important year, because Albania finally becomes independent. Slavko: After the First World War, which was indeed triggered by a Bosnian Serb, the region is redefined and takes the name the Kingdom of Serbs, Croats, and Slovenes. Me, already half-lost and with Isabelle Adjani's nipples sparkling at me all the way from Varennes like two rosy fireflies: What a name. Davor: But ten years later, in 1929, our king, Alexander the First, names it Yugoslavia, which means the land of the southern Slavs. Me: Much better, more poetic. Slavko: And the Macedonians assassinate him in 1934. Davor: But before that, in 1928, they also assassinated Radic, the Croatian independence leader. Slavko: The years of the Second World War are a mess. Davor, smiling: Yes. Slavko: The Italians and Albanians invade Kosovo. Davor: The Bulgarians invade Macedonia. Slavko: The Germans occupy Serbia. Davor: The Italians occupy Montenegro. Slavko, as though praying to a Superman figurine: Josip Broz Tito. And then he said: After the war, in 1945, Tito declares a socialist Yugoslavia that includes the six republics of Croatia, Montenegro, Serbia, Slovenia, Bosnia-Herzegovina, and Macedonia, and that will remain in place until 1991, when finally, after eighty-three years of an artificial union, the whole of Yugoslavia breaks up again. Davor, pressing his thumb and index finger together: Into tiny pieces. Slavko, showing me the palm of his hand: Five new countries. Davor: It could soon be six. Slavko: Or even seven. And the boy reporter,

who so far had been too busy gnawing at his cuticles, raised
his cigarette in the air and drew a picture with the smoke,
saying: At schools all over the Balkan region they teach you
to draw borders on the map with an inkless pen.

Dizzy from the whiskey, or maybe from the overdose of
history, or maybe from something much more ephemeral
or even erotic, I said nothing, although I probably could
have said: The only way to tell a story is to stutter it elo-
quently, or at least that's what a Brooklyn friend who stuttered only when it suited him used to tell me. Or maybe I
could have said: Once, in a hotel in Ilhéus, Lía fell in love
with a hole someone had made in the back of the door of
her room, a deep, inexplicable, sublime hole that she swore
kept getting bigger and deeper every day. Or maybe I could
have said: My grandfather was probably trained by a Polish
boxer in Auschwitz. Or maybe I could have said: I'm back
in the little glass jar again, all mixed up with hundreds
of little blue boys and little pink girls. Or maybe I could
have said: Once, a half-Serbian, half-Gypsy boy wanted to
become a Gypsy musician, and so he said goodbye to his
family, did a pirouette in the middle of a forest, and disappeared forever among the trees of Belgrade. Or maybe I
could have said: Epistrophy doesn't actually mean a fucking thing. But I didn't say anything, luckily.

Davor knocked back what was left of his espresso and,
looking at his watch, said he had to go, that it was already
time to stop by the hotel for another group of architectural
tourists. He didn't smile. I'm going too, said Slavko. My leg's
hurting a bit and I'd rather be lying down. But you two stay,
he added, and then he said something in Serbian to the boy
reporter. I asked Slobodan if he knew the bohemian quarter.

Skadarlija, I read from my notes. That's near where I live, he said. Of course, shouted Slavko with a smile, Eduardo wants to listen to a bit of Gypsy music, and my girlfriend recommended going to the cafés in Skadarlija. Really, you want to hear Gypsy music? Slobodan asked me, but I wasn't sure if he was curious or disapproving, or both. I said I'd buy him a beer if he came with me. Slobodan started mumbling in Serbian, probably that it was already getting late, that they'd be waiting for him at home, that his father needed the suit back. Slavko said something to him in Serbian and gave him a hefty slap on the back, and it was as though he'd unjammed a robot, because Slobodan stopped mumbling immediately and said yes, of course, let's go and hear some Gypsy music.

Skadarlija struck me as more of a decadent neighborhood than a bohemian one, but an attractive sort of decadent, a seductive decadent, like the elaborate speech of a serial killer. We walked for a while. The cold had sharpened and it was still snowing and the snow made everything nobler and more dreamlike and deceptive. Slobodan told me straight out that he hated Gypsies, that most Serbs hated Gypsies, that they were good musicians, sure, but they were also a bunch of fools and lazy slobs. And beggars, he added. Just look at that. There was an old, fat Gypsy woman sitting on the ground with a flaccid breast hanging out. She held out her hand to us while she suckled a baby girl. I gave her a coin, thinking that I'd never have given anything to a Mayan woman breast-feeding in the street, then decided it would be best to forget that thought as soon as possible. Slobodan sighed with distaste.

We went into a little café with no one in it. Then we went into another overlit café that didn't have a name or at least didn't have one written anywhere. The tables were empty. On the bar there were three bottles and maybe a dozen upturned glasses. Slobodan talked to the waiter for a while and then told me we should go, that there was a place farther along that had live music. It's called Nebeski Narod, he said as we crossed the street. It's a Serbian saying, he said. It means people of the heavens, he said. I thought about ethnic cleansing. I thought about racial fanaticisms. I thought about Srebrenica. I thought about the intolerance of any people who think they're the chosen ones, an intolerance that, since my childhood, when they taught me to pray to a God that for some reason spoke only Hebrew, I knew only too well. And as we walked into the People of the Heavens, I smiled at Slobodan as sarcastically as I could.

It was a dark, cramped place that smelled of patchouli oil. We sat down. Slobodan ordered two beers. The musicians will arrive soon, according to the waitress, he said after taking a long swig. I nodded and we stayed quiet for a while as I inspected every person who came through the door. Did you know, Eduardo, that gouging your eyes out, I mean, the expression to gouge your eyes out, means to have an orgasm in Gypsy language? I didn't know, and I didn't think to ask him how he knew. Lick my foot after I've stepped in shit, he said. What? It's a Gypsy insult. Popušiš mi nogu kad stanem u govno. It means lick my foot after I've stepped in shit. Right, I said. Then we reply jedi kurac. But at that moment two Gypsies with trumpets and two Gypsies with violins and another Gypsy with a huge double bass came in and the boy reporter didn't say anything else.

From one corner of the room, they started to play loud and fast and spiritedly, while a girl who had also arrived with them went from table to table with a black hat, asking for money. A kolo, I thought, and then I thought about Lía mounting me and moaning. Proper blues, I thought, proper mariachi music, but without the sadness, or rather with a different form of the same sadness. Because there was sadness in this too, of course, only instead of an open lament, this one was buried and covered up and dressed in too much joy, like a clown's smile.

They played for exactly an hour and we drank three more beers in silence, just listening. The place was pretty full now, mostly with very pale, Gothic-looking Serbian teenagers with piercings hanging from everywhere like stalactites. Slobodan, even though he was more relaxed and had lost the black tie, insisted on keeping up a stoic and indifferent attitude as he sat there biting his nails. Watching him, I had the impression he was someone who had yet to understand that the sea is without doubt the perfect cemetery, and that cowboys always win because they have rifles, and that in fact cowboys always lose because they have rifles, and that honey should be eaten on its own and with your finger and preferably alone, and that the shape of the nipple is far more important than the shape of the breast.

The Gypsies started to file out toward the door as soon as they'd finished. I stood up and told Slobodan I needed his help. I went up to one of the trumpeters, a man in a red jacket and felt hat, and started mumbling something to him, partly in English and partly in Spanish, about a young Gypsy named Milan Rakić, a Gypsy pianist, a friend of mine, and maybe he knew him or had seen him or had heard about him. The trumpeter stood looking at me without saying anything. I took out the photo of Milan and showed it to him. Milan, Milan Rakić, I said, pointing at the picture. With a sickened or perhaps nervous face, Slobodan talked to the Gypsy trumpeter in Serbian, translating what I'd said, and the Gypsy took the photo and looked at it from close up and passed it to his friends and they laughed and the little Gypsy girl laughed and the trumpeter in a red jacket grabbed it back, tearing it a little, and he started shouting at me in Serbian as he jabbed at Milan's face with his index finger and showed me his gold teeth and shouted even louder. He says, Slobodan translated, that the guy in the photo isn't a Gypsy. And still laughing and gesticulating wildly, they walked out.

I stood there a bit disorientated, examining the face in the photo, and Slobodan had to push me back to the table. I'll be right back, he said, throwing me a cigarette and heading for the bar. He doesn't look like a Gypsy because he's got his mother's Serbian features, I said out loud, as though to calm myself down a bit, as though to break the spell, as though to banish the doubt that was starting to loom up all around and gnaw at me like any good film would have done, or any bad film. I lit the cigarette, my hand trembling, or perhaps it wasn't.

Proja, said Slobodan, handing me a plate of something a bit like fried dumplings. And a cold beer, he added. It was warm. We both drank and ate in silence, a private silence amid so much noise and bustle. I had a lot of respect for the way he gave me my space, the way he didn't ask me anything, and maybe because of that, or maybe because I needed to shed a deadweight, I started talking to him about Milan Rakić and San José el Viejo and every postcard he'd sent me before disappearing into a damn myth of his own, and after I don't know how many more little dumplings and beers and cigarettes, I'd told him everything. Slobodan, offering no judgment, left some bills on the table and calmly said let's go, I'm tired.

I got back to the apartment drunk and wide-awake. I turned on the TV. All the channels, or almost all the channels, were showing porn films: some very genteel English ones, some of black men and women with perfect bodies and the stamina of horses, and others that were simple and homemade and badly acted. I always preferred the badly acted ones. I ended up watching a slightly ugly young blond girl who, from time to time, looked at the camera and shouted something and made cartoonish grimaces of pleasure, but then she'd forget that they were fucking her and someone behind the camera would remind her and she'd turn around to look at him with surprise and immediately start up with the almighty shrieking again. And I stayed like that for a long time, spiritually reconciling myself to life.

I slept in. I'd unplugged the phone. I drew the curtains and noticed that, for the first time since my arrival, the sun had come out, but that's really just a figure of speech, because it was still half-overcast. I got dressed quickly. I took the yellow envelope from my suitcase and went out.

Kalemegdan, I said to the taxi driver, showing him the

last postcard. I asked him in Spanish and then in English if it was a park. Park, park, he replied, apparently annoyed.

At the gate was a line of hawkers sitting on the ground, each with a blanket covered with figurines and chinaware and antique coins and prints of Tito and little lace table-cloths and lighters and secondhand hats and who knows what else. I bought a pack of Lucky Strikes. I lit one. I started to walk. It was still cold. The trees were gray and bony and looked like something out of a Tim Burton film. Remnants of the already-melting snow shimmered on the grass like little puddles of milky coffee. I arrived at the banks of the Danube or maybe the Sava, I don't know: I'd been told the two rivers joined right there in Belgrade, in the same way as two great empires had done centuries before. A low stone wall separated the park from the river. I sat down on it and immediately noticed a sour, putrid smell, probably coming from the water. Far off on the other side there was a row of floating houses or something that looked like that. I stubbed my cigarette out on the ground and kept walking. I walked a long way. I reached the for-tress. I glanced at a sign in Cyrillic lettering. To go in, you had to cross a hanging bridge strung over a deep ditch, which in some other time had surely been a pit crawling with hungry crocodiles and dragons. There was nothing but damp inside the ruins, and I hurried on to get out the other side, where in an open field there was an exhibit with tanks and machine guns and armored cars and all kinds of war relics. A pathetic sort of museum, dedicated to the detritus of so many wars.

I sat down on a green bench and, lighting another cigarette, started looking back through Milan's postcards, scrutinizing and rereading them but much less naïvely now, much less passively, looking at them almost as though with a magnifying glass for the slightest detail or fragment or phrase that might shed a bit of light on things, or maybe, given the way things were going, I thought or perhaps even said out loud, throw another handful of darkness over it all. I had read eight or ten or twelve of them when suddenly, as though lost in that sea of postcards, a white card appeared with a drawing of one of Lía's orgasms. The last time, I supposed, before we'd gone to the airport, with her sky blue doctor's outfit thrown on the floor and her scratching my back and arms while telling me not to come, that this time I shouldn't come, and so I hadn't. Saudade, it said in quick, majestic letters above a solitary, fluid black line, a line that ascended and descended symmetrically, and with an odd and unexpected hook at the end. Simple. Elegant. And underneath, in brackets: E boa sorte em Póvoa, meu Dudú. I looked at the drawing carefully, trying to decipher it, but instead I thought about all the lines of Lía's orgasms, about the lines of her body, about the lines on my palm, about the lines that join the stars to form constellations, about the five lines of a musical stave that held Milan back so much, about the lines that unite and divide and reunite the Balkan countries only to divide them again, about the ideological and religious lines that fracture the world and are making it more wretched all the time, and about the tangled web of events and people that, like the tiny dots of a single flourishing sketch, had led me to the banks of some river in Belgrade. I didn't know which river in Belgrade. I understood nothing. I felt superfluous.

As I left the park, I found a welcoming café with a

blackboard in the window announcing the menu of the day in Serbian. I chose a table with a view of the street. The waiter came up and tried to translate the menu for me with gestures and faces and sign language that were no less Serbian. It didn't work. I pointed to the board and nodded boldly and then asked for a coffee. Big, I said to him, holding an invisible balloon in my hands. I lit a cigarette and drank the coffee quickly to warm up a bit. First, a tomato, cucumber and feta salad. Next, a plate of white beans with a couple of sausages on top. Along with my chocolate cake I asked for another coffee and lit another cigarette and spent a while looking out. It was already nighttime. Snow had begun to fall, softly, looking almost fake. A family of Gypsies stopped just outside the window. The boy, who couldn't have been more than four, was crying while his mother told him off in Serbian or Romany. An elderly woman—the boy's grandmother, I suppose—was a few paces ahead, fed up with all the fuss. The father watched in silence, his hands in his overcoat pockets. Come on, the mother ordered the boy, or let's go, or something like that, and she started to walk on, to leave him behind. The Gypsy boy sullenly stayed put. Well, don't come then, she shouted, or something similar, in Serbian or Romany, then let out a snort like a furious bull and carried on walking with the elderly woman, washing her hands of the matter. Entrenched in his stubbornness, the boy didn't move. His father simply looked at him, saying nothing, remaining two or three paces ahead. A standoff. Who will outlast whom. Who is stronger. Which horseman is tougher. They could carry him, I thought as I finished my coffee, make him go with them. They could also leave him until his temper passed and he would have to catch up to them. The two women, unconcerned, were already some way off. Father and son remained three paces apart, not speaking. Suddenly, as the snow was just beginning to whiten them, the father held out his hand to his son, gently. The boy hesitated. Then, with the obligatory reluctance, he took his father's hand, and so they walked away from their stalemate and away from the window. I paid the bill. Quite tired now, I also left.

I was awakened at six in the morning by a hammering on the door. It's me, he shouted, Slobodan. I sighed. I put on a T-shirt and, still in my underwear and half-asleep, opened the door. I was trying to call you yesterday, but you didn't answer, he said as he sat down on the only chair. I sat on the bed, on the pillows. I unplugged the phone, I said, yawning. At that time of the morning, freshly bathed, he looked even more like Bob Dylan. He was wearing the same black suit of his father's, the same black tie. His journalist's uniform, I thought, and I very nearly said it to him. He lit a cigarette, coughing. I closed my eyes for a few seconds, as though to situate myself, and when I opened them, Slobodan was looking at me, perplexed. I made some calls, he told me, and there's no accordionist with the last name Rakić in Belgrade. He threw me the cigarettes. Or at least he's not legally registered under that name, he continued without giving me time to absorb the first blow, because your friend's father could be using a pseudonym or a stage name, which is very common among Gypsies. He took a few drags on his cigarette. I talked to bar and café and restaurant owners, too, and no one knows anything about a pianist named Milan Rakić, which in a way is un-derstandable. You saw yourself the other night how Gypsy musicians arrive in those places and then leave again with-out saying anything, without talking to anyone. Also, yes-terday afternoon I was able to talk to the new director of the classical music conservatory, a friendly Hungarian guy, who told me that the name Rakić wasn't familiar to him but that he'd only been in Belgrade a few months and would consult some colleagues. Slobodan puffed out a mouthful of smoke and said he's a ghost, this Rakić of yours, and he smiled for the first time since I'd met him. He fell quiet then, perhaps waiting for me to talk or explain something. I had nothing to explain. So get dressed, he ordered, we have to get there early. Where do we have to get early? I asked him, standing up and no longer feeling sleepy at all. Sremčica, he said. And what's that? A Gypsy camp, he re-plied. Make sure you bring the photo of your friend. And cigarettes. And plenty of money, too.

It was snowing. From a distance, the houses of Sremčica looked like they were built of cardboard, and some of them probably were. Structures made of sackcloth, scraps of wood, bricks, rusted sheet metal, and anything else that might be on hand and might work: a Latin Ameri-can village through and through. Pick up some stones, said Slobodan, crouching down. I asked him what for, but he didn't hear me or didn't want to answer me or didn't have time, because a few seconds later we already had a pack of wild and rabid dogs running after us and bark-ing and baring their teeth. Just pretend you're going to throw stones at them, he said calmly, cigarette between his lips. And at the first imaginary throw, the dogs stopped barking and left us in peace. How did you know? I asked him when I got my breath back, but he didn't answer. A few Gypsy women were already sweeping up and washing clothes on a patio as some children chased a couple of hens. When they saw us, everyone stopped. It looked as though they were barefoot, even though they weren't. Wait for me here, said Slobodan, and he went to talk to the women. The children couldn't stop touching his black suit. A row of dead animals hung from a clothesline. Rabbits and chickens, I thought. More women started to come out, just women, and I noticed that each time one walked up to the patio, the other women would grab one of her breasts, just like that, casually, as if it was some sort of greeting. I wanted to smile but I was too embarrassed. Slobodan came back. They say we should wait awhile, that he'll be up soon. Who? I asked him. Petar, he said, lighting a cigarette. Do you know him? I asked. A bit, he said, but I doubt he'll remember me. Somewhere in the distance, I heard a groaning sound, like a truck that wouldn't start. I was anxious. I lit a cigarette. At that moment, the first man came out of one of the shacks and headed straight for the trough without saying a word. The second and third men did the same. What's going on? I asked Slobodan. Among the Gypsies, he said, you can't talk to a man in the morning until he's washed his face. I realized that he knew a lot, maybe even too much, for someone who hated Gypsies. Then I realized that, for someone who hated Gypsies, he was also helping me too much. Why are you helping me? I asked him. He didn't say anything for a few minutes, and I'd even forgotten I'd asked the question as I watched one man after another wash his face at the trough and then sit down around the table to drink Turkish coffee, when suddenly Slobodan whispered: I like to know the end of a story. He smiled. And also, he said, you're going to help me with something later. I said I'd be glad to, and guessed that it wouldn't come cheap. Watching the men enjoy their coffee, I wanted one too. That's him, said Slobodan, that one there, the one in the brown coat. He was a short and dark-haired man and, like almost all of them, he had a big mustache. He was wearing a worn-out, wrinkled old suit, and I had the impression he'd even slept in it. I guessed that he was between thirty and forty. One of the women shouted something to him while she pointed at us. The man, his face still wet, walked over slowly. Petar held his hand out to Slobodan, who opened the cigarette pack for him straightaway, and the Gypsy took one. He ignored me until we were introduced. They started talking in Serbian and I heard the truck groaning again, only now it sounded more human, like someone in pain, like someone being tortured. We're going to have breakfast, said Slobodan. And the three of us went out to the street to look for a taxi.

Splavoni. That's what they called the floating houses I'd seen from the park the day before. The area was called Zemun. They were little cafés or restaurants shaped like ferries, and as I looked at them, I started thinking about some Mark Twain novel, or some film by Kim Ki-duk. All very theme park. All very kitsch. With names like Bangkok and Bombardier and Mississippi. Favorite haunts of the Serbian Mafia, Slobodan explained to me as we got out of the taxi in front of one named Savanna, which boasted, and why wouldn't it, a rope bridge and drawings of lions and elephants on the walls and waiters in stupid safari costumes.

Slobodan and I had rolls with cheese and strawberry jam for breakfast and Petar wolfed down a huge slab of grilled meat. No one spoke until the coffees arrived in their little bamboo cups. Then Petar lit a cigarette and asked something in Serbian and Slobodan said go on, show him the photo, and the Gypsy took it and looked at it for a while, shaking his head. He says he's never seen him. He says he doesn't look like a Gypsy musician. He says it's easier to milk a cow when it's standing still. No idea. Without asking me, Petar slipped the photo into the inside pocket of his jacket, and I felt I'd lost it forever. They talked a bit in Serbian. Two thousand dinars, Slobodan said to me, which was about ten dollars. They argued about something for a moment. Another thousand, he added, and I gave him that too. Petar clapped a few times and shouted good, good, and put the cigarettes away in the inside pocket of his jacket. Ridiculous, really, but I suppose the cigarettes and the breakfast were part of the deal. Ask him what it means when a Gypsy does a pirouette, I said to Slobodan. Not now, he said, getting to his feet. I paid for everything and we left.

When we got back to Sremčica, Petar invited us in for a Turkish coffee with his family. Slobodan accepted immediately. If a Gypsy invites you into his house, he said, it's rude to say no. I picked up a stone, but the rabid dogs had disappeared.

Petar's wife was named Casandra. As soon as she saw us, she started cleaning the table and chairs with a damp cloth, somehow scandalized, incessantly complaining or arguing or at least that's what it seemed like. Not once did she look at us. Besh, besh, shouted Petar. Sit down, in Romany, said Slobodan, and we all sat down. There were little flowers painted on the walls. It smelled of nutmeg, laundry, and rubbing alcohol. Sons and daughters-in-law came and went and children ran past and somewhere a baby was crying. All the men were smoking, the boys included. But not the women. The women, with flowery handkerchiefs covering their hair, tended to the men. Dragan, the eldest son, sat down with us. He looked just like his father and was decked out in a huge quantity of gold chains and bracelets. The three of them talked in Serbian and then father and son started to laugh. Petar asked where you're from, explained Slobodan, and I told him Guatemala. I smiled. I helped them to pronounce Guatemala. Casandra brought in some rolls called bogacha and a pot of Turkish coffee and, still grumbling, poured out four little cups. It was strong and sweet and I had another one right away. An old man arrived. He poured himself a cup of Turkish coffee and asked me for a cigarette with his fingers and sat down with us. Sometimes they called him Ursari, sometimes Vodja, sometimes Vashengo, sometimes Bengalo. He didn't talk much and reminded me immediately of Mr. Bojangles, but the tender and tragic Mr. Bojangles of Nina Simone's version. I accepted a black tobacco cigarette from Dragan, which he'd rolled himself. Smoking and listening to them chat in Serbian, I started to think about how this homely and supposedly settled atmosphere also retained an odd sense of the provisional, of the ephemeral, of the transient, and I remembered the Jean Cocteau quote. Suddenly, everyone applauded. I've just asked them what a Gypsy's pirouette means, said Slobodan, and it seems they liked the question. All right, so translate, I said excitedly. Dragan says it's like the Gypsy boy who, one night, could hear his pig squealing and squealing and went out to see what was wrong and grabbed the pig's snout and he found loads of gold coins inside, thousands of gold coins, and then he did a pirouette. Galbi, said Dragan rather proudly as he mimed rubbing coins together with his fingers. Petar shouted something. Petar says Gypsies sometimes do a pirouette before they die. How come? I asked Slobodan. Petar says he saw it once. A long time ago. In the forest. When he still lived in a caravan. He says that all the adults were sitting around a fire telling stories, and he'd lain down and was about to doze off, when he saw a man get up without a word, do a pirouette, and fall down dead next to some trees. Petar says he remembers it as though it had been a dream. We were all quiet, picturing the scene, I suppose. The old man asked something in Romany and then started to tell a story, also in Romany (he didn't speak Serbian or maybe didn't want to speak Serbian), which Petar followed and translated into Serbian and Slobodan translated into English and finally, like the last little deformed doll of a matryoshka, I translated for myself into Spanish. There once was a Gypsy king, he said, whose food was being stolen at night and so, getting worried, he declared that he'd give half his kingdom to whoever managed to watch over and protect his huge store of provisions and delicacies. Is that how you say it, delicacies? Delicacies. The oldest of his three sons told the king not to worry, that he'd do it. And that night, the eldest son lay down in front of the food store, vigilant and holding a dagger or a knife or something like that, I'm not sure how to translate it, but just before dawn, a cool breeze blew in and he fell into a deep sleep, and when he woke up, all the food was gone from the store. The next night, the king's second son sat proudly in front of the doors of the food store, holding an enormous sword, yeah, a sword, but just before dawn a cool breeze blew again and he fell asleep, too, and when he woke up, all the food was gone from the store. The old man stopped and Petar drank his coffee down in one gulp and started shouting at some children who ran past, kicking a ball through the room. The third night, said Slobodan, the king's youngest son promised his father that he'd guard the food, and he sat down in front of the store, but not before he'd lain some tacks or nails on the ground, something like that, something sharp. And just before dawn, when the cool breeze came again and he felt sleepy and laid his head on the tacks or nails or whatever they were, the pain woke him up immediately, and the youngest son saw his gentle little sister, an adolescent girl, come in barefoot and in her night-shirt, then he saw his sister do a single pirouette and, horrified (the old man made a frightened face), he saw his sister's hands turning into axes (the old man raised his hands), and he saw his sister's teeth turning into pointed daggers or knives (the old man showed me what were left of his teeth), and he saw his sister's hair turning into cobras (the old man pulled on his hair), and now fully transformed into a witch, Slobodan translated as the old man and Petar and Dragan laughed, he watched his sister eat up all the food in the store. Silence. Typical, I thought, confusedly shuffling the three stories around in my head, and I asked if that was the end of the story, but everyone's attention had already turned to something else. A girl had appeared with a tray in her hands. She was blond and slim, with a white complexion and green eyes, but a deep green, a Mediterranean green. She looked at us, blushing, put the tray on the table, and walked out. It's hedgehog, said Slobodan, watching her go. It's what? Hedgehog, he repeated while the two Gypsies dug in, using their fingers. They love hedgehog. The last time I came, he said, Petar explained to me that hedgehogs are always tastier in autumn, when they're all chubby and full of fat to get through the winter. He also told me that once they've killed them, the Gypsies hang them up outside overnight, on a clothesline, because they believe that the glow of the moon improves the taste, and then the next day, to get all the spines off, they stick a tube into the dead animal's side and start blowing until they've inflated it completely and they can separate the skin from the bones and pull out all the spines. Try it, he said. It tasted like fish.

We thanked them for the meal. The old man left. Petar and Dragan saw me out and Slobodan arrived a few moments later. It was still snowing. I held out my hand to Petar and he said something to me in Serbian. He says not to worry, translated Slobodan, if your Rakić does exist, he's sure he'll find him for you. I didn't believe him. I could still hear the groaning of the truck or of a person being tortured or something equally horrific. We set off slowly toward the road. The snow creaked under our feet. In the distance, the groaning got louder. What the hell is that? I asked Slobodan, but he just lit another cigarette and kept walking.

Once we were in a taxi, I told him I thought Petar's daughter was gorgeous. The blond girl, I said. The one with the hedgehog, I said. I thought I heard him sigh, though it could have been the wind or else the taxi driver. That's not his daughter, he whispered after a while. It's Dragan's wife. Her name is Natalja. She's my age. We were at school together, until she quit her studies because they made her marry him. She was fourteen then. I thought of asking Slobodan how he knew so much, but there was no need. It was obvious. I rolled the window down a bit and the air was refreshing. It was snowing harder. There was a lot of traffic and we spent more than an hour in complete silence, the two of us probably having the same fantasy or probably having opposite fantasies while we watched the city gradually grow dark.

The next morning it was snowing heavily. The windows were rattling and seemed about to explode. I turned on the TV and watched a whole news bulletin in Serbian, understanding no more than the apocalyptic images of deserted streets and trees blown onto electric cables and blinds of white wind and cars buried in the middle of small mountains of snow. Zdena called. She told me not to worry, that it was best not go to out, that this kind of storm generally lasted a day, two at the most, and that if I needed something, I shouldn't hesitate to call them. I thanked her and we hung up. I looked out the window. No one. Irresistible, I thought. I grabbed my jacket, my gloves, and my hat, and went out.

I was surprised it wasn't colder. It was almost impossible to walk in a straight line. Pellets of snow whipped at my face and neck, and a few times I had to duck behind a phone booth or a lamppost. I passed just one person and we greeted each other like two of those Japanese soldiers who never heard that the war was over and keep wearing their uniforms like total idiots and are still looking for the enemy in the middle of nowhere. The kiosk on the corner was closed. Nearly everything was closed. I kept walking down Pozeska Street. I could make out a red light in the window of a bar or café, but the door was locked. I rapped on it. A moment later, a woman arrived and said something to me through the glass and I shrugged and said hvala, which means thanks, and had nothing to do with anything, but it was the only Serbian word that came to mind. Scornfully, and at snowstorm prices, she sold me a liter of beer, a piece of smoked sausage, a bread roll, and a pack of cigarettes. Hvala, I said again, and walked back to the apartment, feeling strangely happy.

I spent the rest of the day shut inside, smoking and eating the supplies I'd bought and reading a bit and listening to a few pieces by Melodious and watching Venezuelan soaps dubbed into Serbian, and Russian films dubbed into Serbian, and American cartoons dubbed into Serbian, and taking short naps without dreaming or at least dreaming very little, and it was one day less, one day lost, one day further from everything and closer to nothing, while the hours didn't pass so much as suddenly become one single hour, one single static hour like a bedsheet with no creases, one goddamn shitty and unbelievably eternal hour, so dark and so lonely and tasting of dead birds.

It's passed, Slavko said to me over the phone, as though I'd had a fever. Maybe I did have a fever. It was nine in the morning. Outside, the wind had stopped moaning. I drew the curtains and saw that it had stopped snowing, too, but it was still overcast. Yes, I said, it's passed. Are you leaving soon? he asked. Yes, soon, and I closed my eyes melodramatically, trying to imagine myself already in the warmth of Portugal. Slavko said I should have lunch with them, that a really crazy friend of his from Vojvodina was coming, and he wanted to introduce me. Sure, thanks, I said, and then, although I don't know why, I went back to sleep for a few hours.

I left the building toward midday and was looking for a taxi—from any company, of course—when I heard someone shouting my name. It was Slobodan. Without the black suit, finally, and his hair even more messy and disheveled. He had the eyes of a man who hadn't slept. This is for you, he said without even greeting me, handing me a piece of paper. Gardoš, I read, confused. It's the name of a district, he said. On the other side of the river. Petar says he can't be sure you'll find anything but that you should try walking around there. Gardoš, I repeated. A district. Is that it? I asked, and feeling frustrated, I crumpled the piece of paper and put it in my jacket pocket. And the photo of Milan? I asked, but Slobodan was looking at something else and I thought he was about to cry. He just sighed. I need your help, he said, biting his nails and looking at me as if I were guarding life's great secret. I don't know if Natalja had been standing there all along or if she'd just arrived or if perhaps I'd decided not to see her—but there she was, all rosy and sad. And I suddenly remembered a legend Lía had told me, studious and devoted to quantum physics as she was. The legend says that as Columbus's fleet was approaching the shores of America, the native Indians didn't see it because they couldn't see it, they literally couldn't see it, since the concept of galleons in full sail was so alien to them, so unimaginable, that it didn't enter into their version of reality, and as such, their minds simply decided not to register it. There's nothing there, I remember Lía saying to me, with her hand on her forehead, as though she was watching the horizon. I construct my reality solely on the basis of that which I know, she said. Or something like that. I need your help, Slobodan said to me again, and I stood looking at them and somehow inserted them into my new reality. They were like two teenagers skipping class. I wanted to hug them. Slobodan was quiet. Natalja, without seeing me, said a word in Romany that had a beautiful sound, like a goldfinch's trill, but I didn't know what it meant and foolishly didn't ask. I understood everything else, though. I told Slobodan of course, no problem, that I wouldn't be back till late, and gave him the key to the apartment. I started to go, somehow both satisfied and also rather melancholy. Hey, he shouted, and I stopped. According to Natalja, he said, gesturing at her with his chin, doing a pirouette doesn't mean anything to Gypsies. I know, I was going to say, but I just smiled.

When I got to the Lecićs' house, a man with long gray hair and a goatee—the whole musketeer look—opened the door. I'm Neboyša Tuka, he said to me in English. I held out my hand. Have you brought the buffalo's milk? he asked me. I didn't say anything. Go and buy us a liter of buffalo's milk, he said. I started to step back, a little afraid. Slavko appeared at the door on his crutches and, pushing him aside, said stop fucking around, Neboyša.

Marko had spread on the table all sorts of nuts, cheeses, sausages, hard-boiled eggs sliced in half and served with coarsely ground pepper, a tomato salad, and a casserole of chopped vegetables and something spicy called ajvar. They poured a few glasses of beer. As we ate, Neboyša talked about Vojvodina and about his chauffeur, who was waiting outside for him, and he kept glancing out the window. I think my anxiety was sparked when I tried a bite of the apple tart, although when I think about it, that's not right at all, because the anxiety was always there, but well camouflaged. Neboyša asked me something and, I don't know why, I said yes. I drank half a glass of warm beer as an anesthetic. I was sweating. I felt the crumpled piece of paper in my pocket and became even more anxious. Gardoš, I whispered, as though to calm myself down. While she made the Turkish coffee, Zdena asked me if I'd been to Knez Mihajlova. It's a really lovely pedestrianized street, she said, there are loads of restaurants and cafés with terraces. I don't know, maybe, I replied, remembering the two Gypsy siblings dancing between the tables of a Degas painting. I lit a cigarette. I think you'd like it, she said. Neboyša said something in Serbian. Everyone laughed. They're saying, Zdena explained to me as she sat down, that Knez Mihajlova is where everyone goes to be seen, all clean-shaven and dolled up and wearing their best clothes and their best shoes, even though they haven't got two pennies to rub together. It's ridiculous, added Neboyša. They spend all their money on some rip-off outfit and some rip-off coffee, when they don't even have food to eat at home. Seventy percent of Belgrade is chronically depressed, said Slavko, and I wanted to ask him how he'd arrived at that number, but Marko, who until then had been quiet and pensive, started to tell me the story of a neighbor who used to beat a chopping board with a wet rag in the evenings. What for? I asked, finishing my coffee. So that we'd all think she was tenderizing a piece of meat, he said. She didn't have the money to buy meat anymore, obviously, but it still mattered to her that her neighbors thought she did. Just like that lot on Knez Mihajlova, said Slavko. You see them walking around and having a coffee and laughing and they pretend they're doing just fine, that they're happy, that they've got money, but the truth is, they've built this glittering facade of clothes and makeup to hide the fact that they're dead inside, to look the other way from the scars left by the war. Like the bombed-out buildings, I said without thinking about it much, and everyone looked at me in silence and no one said anything else after that.

I asked Zdena to call me a taxi so I could get to Gardoš. Ah, Gardoš is lovely, she said. There's a tower, Eduardo. Make sure you go up the tower. You can see the whole city from there. Neboyša asked for another taxi to go back to Vojvodina. I looked at him, confused, and as we both walked out, I asked him about his chauffeur. What chauffeur?

Dusk had fallen when I got to Gardoš. All the streets were narrower and steeper and the Austro-Hungarian influence was obvious on this side of the river. I was still feeling anxious, and for some reason I was expecting to run into Milan at any moment, right there, hanging around on a street corner or sitting on a bench, and I started looking closely at everyone, scrutinizing them as they walked past. I forgot his face for a few seconds and had to concentrate to recall it. Pale, I said to myself. Long, shiny black hair, I said.

A nocturnal gaze, I said, and probably smiled stupidly. I passed by a landau or something that in the darkness looked like a landau. I passed by a guy dressed like a pimp, and maybe he was a pimp, but with no whores in sight. I realized then that Gardoš was a very quiet cobblestoned neighborhood, and walking among the old houses and the lights that looked like gas lamps and through a thick blanket of fog, I felt plunged into the eighteenth century, maybe the nineteenth, and I suddenly had the feeling that I was the lost one and someone else was looking for me, that someone else was following me. I stopped and rather ridiculously looked back and decided there wasn't anyone there, even though I now know very well that there was.

I went into a bar. It was empty and the waiter didn't fill me with confidence. Then I went into a small restaurant, but no one spoke English. I kept walking. A little way off, at the top of a steep street, a group of people stood in a circle by a lamppost. I thought that in the middle of the circle there might be a Gypsy musician, an accordionist or perhaps a violinist, and I slowly began walking over. As I approached, I could make out six or seven men, all with cropped hair, black boots, thick chains, and leather jackets. They fell quiet as they watched me walk up the street. When I was closer to them, I looked up so that I could prove my passivity with a smile, and I noticed that one of them had a green or maybe black swastika tattooed on his neck. I felt sick. I quickened my pace. They shouted something in Serbian, but I ducked into a bar and went up to the counter and asked for a vinjak, which was the cheap whiskey, and lit a cigarette. Slowly, the sickness or fear or whatever it had been started to fade. At the other end of the bar, a fat guy was drinking something and reading the paper. I asked the barman if he spoke English. He shook his head, shrugged his shoulders, and started jabbering incoherently. The fat guy lowered his paper and shouted that he spoke English, then asked what I wanted. I'm looking for somewhere with Gypsy music, I said, and he translated it for the barman, who answered fully, complete with jerks and gestures. Says there's not much around these parts, but you can try a couple of cafés where they usually turn up. And even though he mentioned the names, they didn't stay with me. He held his arm out and said that I should turn right out of the door (the neo-Nazis were to the left) and walk three hundred meters and both places were just there, right across from each other. I thanked him, finished my whiskey, and paid. The neo-Nazis had gone, but I imagined them waiting for me around some corner, knives in hand. I followed the route and probably got lost, because I didn't find anything. The little streets were tightly wound and they all looked alike, and who the hell's going to count exactly three hundred meters? I went into a corner shop. I bought cigarettes and a packet of chewing gum, and a short, thin, friendly Chinese man came outside with me and showed me how to get there.

Only one of the two cafés was open. I realized as I went in that calling it a café was a bit generous. Sitting around one of the two tables, smoking and drinking Turkish coffee and talking loudly, were three Gypsy men. All wore striped polyester suits. Their three felt hats were lined up on the table. They ignored me. The woman in charge didn't speak English either, and I ordered a vinjak. I lit a cigarette. The Gypsies were talking loudly and clapping their hands as though there was no one else in the whole world, and in their world there probably wasn't. One of them looked different from the other two, darker or perhaps more Arabic. Suddenly, all three of them sipped from their coffees at the same moment, and I took advantage of the silence to ask them if they spoke English. The three of them, waving their hands excitedly, said they didn't and told me not to bother them, and so, I don't know why, I said bueno, gracias, and one of them, the more Arabic-looking one, looked up, and I knew straight away that he'd understood. Do you speak Spanish? I asked. Yep, that I do, kid, he shouted in an Andalusian accent. From Seville? I asked. No way, he said, laughing, not from anywhere. But yeah, I spent some time in a village very close to Seville. He spoke a heavy, lethargic Spanish, as though he was dragging the syllables behind him. He asked me if I was from Spain and I said no, from Guatemala. From Guatemala, he repeated with surprise, and then he told his friends and the three of them laughed for a while. And what's a kid from Guatemala doing around here? On holiday, I said. I drank the vinjak down in one gulp and ordered another. And do you live in Belgrade? No, no. In Čukarička Padina. It's a little way away, in the country, he said, standing up and taking one of my cigarettes without asking and without saying thank you, even though they had a few packs of their own on the table. As though all cigarettes were communal property. He stood there. They call me Bebo, he said, holding out his hand. He had a big scar on his bald head. Can I buy you a drink, Bebo? I asked, and he shouted something to the woman, who immediately brought a glass and filled it with a thick, cold vodka. Looking up at him, I told Bebo I was there in Gardoš to try to find a bit of Gypsy music. My two friends are trumpeters, he said, gesturing at them with his glass of vodka. He said something to them in Romany and then, a bit suspiciously, asked me why there, why Gardoš. I weighed my words carefully, or maybe I didn't. I'm looking for a Gypsy pianist, I said. Petar from Sremčica sent me, I said. His two friends understood me or at least understood the name Petar and the word Sremčica and started shouting and gesticulating with annoyance. Bebo seemed to be calming them down. He asked me how I knew Petar from Sremčica, but I didn't have time to reply. His two friends were standing now, holding their black instrument cases, which I instinctively imagined to be covered with pictures of naked Thai women on the inside. I stood up too. Please, I said, and I don't know how, but I managed to hear the sound of myself saying it, a pathetic, foreign sound, like when you hear a recording of your own voice. He downed his vodka and started talking with them in Romany. Got any money? he asked, and I said yes, of course, however much it takes, and then I regretted saying that. All right, he said, they're going over there, but they say you definitely won't be allowed in. It's only for Gypsies. I wanted to ask where they were going. I kept my mouth shut. How much money you got? I handed him a five-thousand-dinar bill. More, for my friends, he said plaintively, and I handed him another five thousand. They shared the money between them. I'm not going, he said. My friends will take you, so follow them, but they insist you won't be allowed in, all right? Bebo shouted something to the woman and she rushed out and poured a little more of the cold vodka into his glass. There was a silence that was too long. Bebo, have you ever heard of a Gypsy suddenly doing a pirouette? A what? What does it mean when a Gypsy suddenly does a pirouette? I said. Bebo shook his head. A pirouette? I don't know, kid. There are some Manouche Gypsies, in France, who never stop doing pirouettes. They jump forward and backward and all around, like little frogs or something. I don't know why they do it. He asked his friends and they said something to him, laughing. They say that if a Gypsy does a pirouette, it means that Gypsy's crazy. And Bebo laughed hard. His friends walked out. I'd like to go with you, he said, but I got a warm woman waiting for me. Yekka buliasa nashti beshes pe done grastende, we say in Romany. It means that you can't sit on two horses with one backside.

They walked eight or ten paces in front of me, quickly and without so much as looking to check whether I was following them. I was nervous, and a few times I thought about stopping or running away or finding a taxi to take me back to the safety of the apartment. We passed the Gardoš tower. Then we passed a little park and I thought I saw a white horse tied to the trunk of a tree, bending its head to graze. Impossible, I thought, Bebo's last words still echoing in my head. But the white shape in the night was still there. At some point, it started to snow. It seemed we left Gardoš and then it seemed we left Zemun and then, somehow, it seemed we left Belgrade. But I could still make out the putrid smell of the Danube or the Sava, which-ever it was, and so I was able to orient myself, and for a few blocks we didn't see a single person. No one. We walked into a dark alley and, of course, they soon stopped.

I reached them. One of them asked me for a cigarette by tapping his fingers to his lips. As he lit it, the other felt my jacket and said something in Serbian or maybe in Romany. Then they kept walking and, who knows why, I followed four paces behind them, as if I were being dragged along by some strange tide. I also lit a cigarette, trembling a little. I blew out a mouthful of cold smoke. Sometimes, I suppose, hope is stronger than fear.

We arrived at a huge rusty door in what felt like an industrial district. There was no light. There was no sign. There wasn't a soul on the street. There was no sound. No music, no voices, nothing. The snow kept falling. One of them banged hard on the door and shouted something incomprehensible at me, and I thought again about making a run for it. They both laughed. Suddenly, I heard the door creaking. A huge mustachioed man dressed in black appeared through the opening and greeted the two Gypsies, kissing them on the cheeks. He stood looking at me. The two Gypsies started explaining why I was there and he shook his head, as though disappointed, while making a clicking sound with his tongue that in every language in the world means no. One of the Gypsies said something to me, something that probably meant: see, we told you. And the guy in black let them past. Dinars, I said, taking out some bills, probably too many bills, and the guy snatched them from me irritably. Then he shouted something, spat a gob of phlegm at the ground (although it was dark, so I couldn't be sure), and shut the door with a single shove.

I was alone, lost in the middle of who knows where, and almost out of money. It was still snowing. I clenched my jaw to keep from shivering, and maybe to keep from crying. I folded my arms. I lit a cigarette and tried to imagine what was on the other side of the door. I couldn't imagine anything. I told myself it was probably an abandoned warehouse or a textile factory or just a big rusty door for screwing money out of stupid, credulous tourists. I shut my eyes and, just for a moment, from far off, I thought I heard music. But no. Nothing. Just my imagination.

Twenty or thirty minutes later, the door opened again. The guy in black put his head out and shouted something at me and then went quiet, apparently waiting for a reply. What d'you want? I said in Spanish, raising my gloved hands toward the sky. I thought of giving him my money. I thought of running into the building. He shouted at me again, still furious, still waiting for a reply. I don't know from where, and I don't know why, but Stravinsky and San Francisco and the Golden Gate Bridge came into my mind and so, without even thinking it through, I said to the guy I phuv kheldias. His face softened. He didn't smile, but nearly. Earthquake, I whispered to him in Spanish, my favorite postcard. I phuv kheldias, he said, as though helping me to pronounce it correctly. I said it again, offering him a cigarette. He took the whole pack, and still kind of annoyed, said I phuv kheldias, I phuv kheldias, like that, twice, as though it was some secret key. Then he moved to one side and, with a generous sweep of his hand, invited me in.

It was darker inside than out. I shook the snow off myself. Nervously, I started to walk forward. I looked back, asking him for help or reassurance or something, and the guy in black, with another movement of his hand, indicated that I should just keep going forward. And so I kept walking, slowly, terrified, feeling as if I were in a film, but I wasn't sure what kind. A romance film, I thought. A thriller, I thought. I could feel the unfathomable emptiness around me, the total absence of everything. The only sound was the metal sheeting of the roof as it crashed against the rafters. Suddenly, the darkness deepened and my steps became shorter, clumsier, and more hesitant. I put my arms out, expecting to find at any moment a wall, a door handle, a person, something, anything I could touch. I sighed and thought I heard the echo of my own sigh. Then I thought I heard the scuttling of a rat. Then I thought I heard a shout. Then I thought I heard a bit of music hidden in some distant hissing. But no. I wanted to talk, to say something, in order to feel part of the world again, but in that situation words didn't belong to me anymore. I had gone beyond language. Beyond any rational concept. Beyond myself. Beyond any understanding of what was happening. Beyond any god or doctrine or gospel or borderline between one thing and another. Just beyond.

My hands quickly came up against something. I banged hard with my fist, almost desperately, and a heavy door opened right in front of me, a door I hadn't even suspected was there. And before I knew it, I was inside and the door had shut behind me. I didn't have time to decide anything. When it's important, when it really matters, you never have time to decide anything.

I stayed still, trying to figure out where I was, what I'd gotten myself into. But there was too much smoke, and a faintly orange light like the dawn. It was a large, hot room.

There were Gypsies standing, others leaning against walls or sitting on plastic or leather chairs. They were drinking. They were smoking. They were talking loudly. The ceiling was very low and the few yellowish lightbulbs were strung up like little hanged men, bouncing gently from the commotion or perhaps just out of habit. Everything had a sepia glow to it, but a weathered, opaque sort of sepia. In the main room were some steps going up and a number of passageways with small doors that people went in and out of as though it were part of some dubious game. Some Gypsies shouted something to me. I smiled at them and started to walk aimlessly through the smoky yellowish light. I realized (or I realize now) that the whole scene was shaded with a sort of forbidden tinge, a secretive tinge, the tinge of a speakeasy in 1930s Harlem. There was smoke everywhere, as though flooding over us, as though drowning us, as though everything were made of smoke, begun in smoke.

Sitting in a corner, an old man wearing rags and with an elfin face was holding his drink. He beckoned for me to come over. I hesitated, and the old man summoned me again. I walked slowly toward him. His teeth were black. He asked me something in Romany. Music, I said to him. He frowned. Music, music. The old man started to laugh. He shouted something. I felt watched by everyone else, and I don't know why, but until then I hadn't realized that there were only Gypsy men around me, not a single woman. The old man handed me his glass and, with another gesture of his hands, told me to drink. It tasted of brandy. I gave him the glass back and he continued talking to me as though I understood him. I shrugged. He clapped a few times and at that moment, from way off somewhere, from a different room, the sound of a piano started up. I stood there quietly. Was it a piano? It was definitely a piano. I excused myself with a weak smile.

I walked slowly through the room and then down one of the passages until I got to a half-closed door. I could still hear the muted sound of the piano. I opened the door and, dimly, like in a faded dream or in a faded dream sequence from an old film, I saw a woman putting on her makeup or brushing her hair in the mirror. She turned toward the door and stuck her tongue out at me, and I felt a primal sort of fear and slammed the door and walked back a few paces and nearly fell over. At the end of the passage, a man with gray hair shouted something at me. He looked angry. I ignored him. Without thinking about it, I tried to open another door, but it was locked. The gray-haired man carried on insulting me. I managed to open a smaller door. It was a lightless room, or rather one with only the frail glow of a solar eclipse. It smelt of hashish, of gangrene, of wet laundry. Sitting on a stool, a plump red-haired girl with her freckled breasts out was putting her stockings back on. She smiled, gestured for me to come in, her mouth open, with the look of a slippery rattlesnake, and it dawned on me that I was in a brothel. Was I in a brothel?

I went back into the main room. The old man was still there. He gave me his glass again and I drank all the brandy while he and the others made fun of me. I didn't mind much. I could still hear the piano. I was feeling a bit dizzy. I tried to ask him where the music was coming from, but he just smiled his rotten smile and clapped a few times. Piano, I shouted. Where's the piano? Upstairs? I pointed, and he, his hand festooned with gold rings and chains, signaled to me that I should go ahead, go on up.

The stairs were steep. I started to climb up, but as I did so the sound of the piano appeared to be descending the stairs. Like a cat going down eighty-eight steps. Like it was looking for me. I reached a mezzanine or a landing with a number of closed doors. The ceiling was even lower here and the walls were painted burgundy and there was a single yellow lightbulb hanging in the middle, swinging. I crouched down. I felt hypnotized. Comatose, even. Straddling some nonexistent and probably dangerous border. But the piano was still playing. Yes, there it was, the tinkling of the piano. Close by. I could hear its tune, but I couldn't find it. An invisible tune, I thought. An ethereal tune, I thought. It had to be Milan.

I opened one of the doors. Sitting on the edge of a rickety old bed was a very pale girl with lank black hair and big blue eyes. She seemed to be fifteen or sixteen from where I stood, but she could have been older. She had the look of someone who had just been crying. She was wearing a long turquoise skirt and a very light sleeveless white blouse. She was barefoot. Her skin shone, maybe with sweat, although I doubt it. On her wrists and ankles she wore thin chains made of fake gold coins. She looked at me sternly, almost sadly, and I don't know why, but I stood still, holding the door handle. Suddenly, and in silence, she got up and walked slowly toward me. She put her cold hand on mine and both our hands closed the door together and then the sound of the piano faded a little. She was taller than I'd thought. I felt her face close to my face and I inhaled her breath, which smelled like rain, or perhaps it smelled like mandarins, and in her eyes I saw all the sensuality of a Gypsy woman. I heard the piano again and started to smile out of sheer nervousness. She placed her hands on my chest and pushed me into the wall. She pressed herself against me. Now her fingers were gently caressing my cheeks, my neck, my stomach; they were finding their way into my pockets and rummaging until they reached my money, maybe the last of it. I felt dizzy, feverish, and sometimes what reigns is confusion, and sometimes confusion holds the reins. She perched her little Gypsy feet on top of mine. I felt the warmth of her crotch on mine. I shut my eyes hard and put my hands on the ceiling to hold myself steady, to hold it all steady, and I listened to the muffled piano and felt how the girl's damp hands slid down my neck and my torso, and at that moment I thought about the Gypsies' third talent, which is a secret, and I thought about pirouettes, about all those pirouettes, and I thought that the lines of my life had been drawn to diverge at that moment, right there, at that very point, at that very second, in front of that turquoise, spectral Gypsy, and suddenly, through the cloud of smoke, I thought I saw Milan's father's face, which at the same time was my own father's face, calling me in Romany or maybe in Hebrew and holding out one of his hands so that I'd take it and he could help me. The fingers of the young girl inserted themselves expertly into my pants. I opened my eyes. With my hands still on the ceiling, I put my mouth to her marzipan cheek. I wanted to tell her something, anything. But suddenly she was on her knees. She whipped my pants down almost violently, sank all the warmth of her face into me, and looked up at me beseechingly with her big sky blue eyes. The piano, I whispered in a Spanish that sounded too lascivious, trembling and smiling euphorically while feeling judged by such blue eyes, and then I thought I heard, far off, as though subliminally, as though tangled up, as though it came from inside me, as though threaded through the rest of that music and all the music of the universe, one of the syncopated melodies of Melodious Thunk. Impossible to know which one. Better that way.

A Speech at Póvoa

A few weeks ago, I got an e-mail notifying me of the subject of this conference, "A Literatura Rasga a Realidade," "Literature Tears Through Reality," a very beautiful phrase but one that ultimately left me no more enlightened than I'd been to begin with. The first thing I did, after having spent a few minutes scratching my bald head, was write to Manuela Ribeiro, the director of the Correntes d'Escritas Festival, to solicit her help, and to ask her if the subject was the intersection between literature and reality, or rather the way literature bursts into reality, or what? And she wrote back to me right away: Yes, that's it. The second thing I did, having seen the names of my fellow speakers, was to write to João Paolo Cuenca, asking him to please explain it to me, this matter of how it is that literature tears through reality. But my Brazilian friend—just as confused or nervous as I was, or perhaps already at work on his own fifteen-minute speech—didn't take long to reply: I have no idea either. So, later that night, I sat down to watch an Ingmar Bergman movie, hoping to distract myself a little. But when it was over, when I wanted to sleep, the subject of this conference returned to assail me again, and I tossed and turned in my bed. Now desperate, at about five or six o'clock on a very cold morning, my thoughts returned to the Bergman movie and I realized that right there, at the conclusion of the movie, was my answer. That, however, is the ending to my fifteen minutes, and it is best to begin at the beginning.

I suspect that my insomnia was provoked by the subject of reality—even though at that time, I should add, I was also suffering great anxiety in an attempt to obtain a tourist visa for Belgrade, going through bureaucratic procedures of kafkaesque proportions in order to visit that agreeable city where, before coming here to Póvoa do Varzim, I've just spent a few days in pursuit of a ghost.

What is reality? I don't know. How do I conceive of reality? No idea. But fortunately I understood that this wasn't to be an epistemological conference, and so, thank God, I was able to discard immediately any reflections on our awareness of reality. And so I came to this strange verb: rasga. I presumed, stumbling through the darkness, that the verb rasgar means the same in Portuguese as in Spanish, and setting aside its musical sense—in Spanish, to rasgar a guitar is to strum it—I focused on the act of breaking something, cutting it, ripping it, tearing it into pieces. I can remember imagining three things. One: someone tearing (rasgando) a piece of cloth. Two: a broken (rasgado) car window. And three: the noise made when you tear (rasga) a sheet of paper in half. With these images as my starting point (when I write, or when I want to understand anything, which is almost the same thing, I always start from images), I asked myself how it was possible for literature to rasgar reality, to break or tear it. As though reality were a piece of cloth? As though reality were a car window? As though reality were a sheet of paper? And it occurred to me that the only possible way of understanding something, or at least of making an attempt or some movement toward understanding it, is to turn to one's own experience. Like so: What link is there, in my experience as a writer, between literature and reality? Or like so: How has my literature torn through reality? The process is always one from a hot furnace to the finger to the brain to the scream. In other words, by induction.

I thought then, inevitably, of the story of my Polish grandfather in Auschwitz. A story that, until he told it to me, nobody in my family knew. When he arrived in Guatemala after the war, he clammed up completely. He refused to talk about the time he'd spent in the various concentration camps. But a few years ago, six or seven years, perhaps, I somehow dared to ask him if I could interview him. To learn a bit, to find out, to leave some record (not to mention evidence) so that I could perhaps then tell the story myself. And my grandfather, with absolute calm, said sure, gladly. We agreed on the day and the time, and I managed to borrow a video camera. I filmed him talking—for the first time in almost sixty years—about his capture at Łódź while he was playing dominoes with some friends, about the last time he saw his family, about his passage through the various concentration camps, about the Polish boxer who, he told me, saved his life in Auschwitz. And this short, simple story of the Polish boxer seemed powerfully literary to me. It goes something like this. My grandfather is in the Sachsenhausen concentration camp. He accepts the gift from a new prisoner of a twenty-dollar gold coin, which he will use to get more food, more soup. They find him out, beat him, and send him to Block Eleven at Auschwitz, to be shot against the already-infamous Black Wall. That night—the night before being put on trial—he's thrown into a cell filled with people, and there he meets a Polish boxer. They speak the same language. They're from the same town. The Polish boxer is still alive because the German soldiers like watching him box, presumably (with a certain amount of license) rather like watching a cockfight. An old, experienced resident of Auschwitz's Block Eleven, the Polish boxer spends the whole night telling my grandfather what to say and what not to say at his trial the following day. Training him, as it were, with words. And the following day, my grandfather says and doesn't say what the Polish boxer told him to say and not to say, and this does indeed save him. The end. I liked this story straight away, perhaps for its simplicity or its apparent simplicity, perhaps for what it implies about the use of words for salvation, for our salvation. I already had the reality—I even had it on film. And now I needed to bring it over into literature. But how to recount this reality? From what point of view? From what moment in time? I tried in many different ways, and using many different narrative techniques, until finally, six or seven years after I'd walked away with this story under my arm (as a friend of mine would describe it in his apartment on Conde de Xiquena), I managed to write a piece in which a grandson interviews his grandfather about his experiences in Auschwitz while he's looking at the five green numbers on his arm and they're drinking a bottle of whiskey together. And that was it. All done. I had managed to carry reality over into literature. I had managed, through literature, to penetrate reality. All lovely and perfect and smelling of printer's ink. Until recently. One morning, I opened the Sunday supplement of a Guatemalan newspaper, and even before I'd managed to take my first sip of coffee, I saw a photo of my grandfather on his butter-colored leather sofa, showing those five pale numbers and saying in an interview that he'd been saved in Auschwitz thanks to (I had to read it twice) his skills as a carpenter.

What? A carpenter? What skills as a carpenter? What happened to the Polish boxer, to Scheherazade in disguise?

And that's it.

Literature is no more than a good trick a magician or a sorcerer might perform, making reality appear whole, creating the illusion that reality is a single unified thing. Or perhaps literature needs to construct one reality by destroying another—something that in a very intuitive sense my grandfather already knew—that is, by destroying and then reconstituting itself from its own debris. Or perhaps literature, as my old friend from Brooklyn used to argue, is no more than the precipitate, zigzagging, rambling discourse of a stutterer.

It was something like this that I was reasoning out and brooding over during that cold, sleepless dawn, just about to understand or at least to find something important, when all of a sudden, now smoking a cigarette in bed, I remembered Ingmar Bergman.

The movie is called *Skamme* in Swedish, *Shame* in English, *Vergonha* in Portuguese. And it's about the experience of a musician couple who take refuge on an island during the Swedish civil war, but being Bergman, it's also much more than that. It goes something like this. Having lost everything—their house, their belongings, their marriage, their dignity, even their shame—the couple board a boat full of refugees trying to flee the island and the war. The boat's engine fails and they are stranded in the middle of the sea. They share the last pieces of bread, the last lumps of sugar, the last drops of water. One man kills himself. The boat gets trapped—in a marvelously horrific image—surrounded by a mass of floating corpses. And in the final scene, the beautiful Liv Ullmann, in a laconic, lost voice that anticipates her death, tells us of a dream she's had. She says: I had a dream. I was walking down a lovely street. On one side, the houses were white, with large arches and columns. On the other side, there was a shady park. Between the trees ran a brook of dark green water. At last I reached a high wall covered in roses. And a plane passed by and set fire to the roses. But nothing happened, because it was a beautiful image. I looked at the water and saw the reflection of how the roses burned. I was carrying a little girl in my arms. Our daughter. She hugged me close. I could even feel her mouth against my cheek. The whole time I knew there was something I mustn't forget. Something that somebody had told me. But I forgot it.

That is exactly what literature is like. As we write, we know that there is something very important to be said about reality, that we have this something within reach, just there, so close, on the tip of our tongue, and that we mustn't forget it. But always, without fail, we do.

Sunsets

My grandfather's body was a vague shape on the bed. I could see it from the doorway, face-up, rigid, quite small, totally covered by his maroon-and-black-checkered quilt. It was Saturday. He'd died early that Saturday morning while he and my grandmother were sleeping. It was forbidden, until dusk, until the end of the day, to move or to touch this small, vague shape that a few hours earlier had been my grandfather.

I entered the bedroom slowly, trying to detect the smell of death. But it didn't smell of anything, or it didn't smell of anything other than the medicines and ointments and the sedentary air that always accompanies the elderly. My grandmother was seated on the far side of the bed—that is, on her side of the bed—with her back to my grandfather's body. I thought she seemed much more stooped now. Her eyes downcast, she held a bag of ice on her left knee. Facing my grandmother was a fat, bald man with a disheveled red beard, dressed in black except for a cream-colored shirt. He was seated in a chair that clearly didn't belong in my grandparents' bedroom and that someone had probably brought in that morning. The man adjusted his skullcap and greeted

178

me with a nod but said nothing, his face set in a permanent grimace. I walked over to him. He got up straightaway and offered me a doughy hand. My condolences, he whispered in poor Spanish and I don't know why, maybe it was my nerves, maybe it was the huge effort he made to sound solemn, but I let out a small laugh. Solemnity, among strangers, is always farcical. He became even more serious and was about to say something to me or ask something of me, when my grandmother finally looked up. Leibele, she stammered, reaching out for my hand. That's what she called my grandfather, Leibele, which is León in Yiddish. I crouched down, gave her a kiss and then a hug, and my grandmother held my hand between hers, gripping it tightly, clinging to it as though it were a buoy at sea, it occurred to me then, as I began to feel slightly dizzy and noticed that the bag of ice was about to slip and fall on the carpet. I asked what had happened to her knee. My grandmother tried to say something to me but couldn't and just managed to purse her lips.

You should put this on, the man said to me somewhat brusquely, handing me a white skullcap. Out of respect, he said as I stood looking at the white skullcap in my hand. Kipa, in Hebrew. Yarmulke, in Yiddish. Respect for whom? I thought of asking. But I just put it on. Sit, sit, he said. He moved to one side and pointed to the chair and I thanked him. The chair was warm.

My grandmother whispered something, as though to herself, as though merely to make her presence felt, and carried on lightly shaking her head. She remained anchored to my hand. The bag of ice still sat precariously on her knee.

She had the dull, abstracted gaze of someone who had been given a few sedatives.

Shlomo, said the man. I looked up. I tried to focus but all I could see was that his reddish beard, around his mouth, was full of biscuit crumbs. I'm Shlomo, the rabbi, the man said. We haven't met, he said, you and I, and maybe he noticed that I was looking at his dirty, matted beard, because he immediately rubbed it and crumbs fell like snowflakes onto the carpet. But I know who you are. The grandson, he said. The artist, he said, and I felt a bit insulted and didn't know if he was confusing me with my brother, but I was too lazy to ask or correct him, so I just said yeah, that's me.

He spoke slowly, the rabbi, haltingly, with a heavy foreign accent. Possibly a Yiddish or an Israeli accent. It occurred to me that maybe he was the new rabbi, since in a Jewish community as small as Guatemala's (a hundred families, they usually say), the rabbis are always imported. I remember that when I was a child, there was a rabbi from Miami Beach, more serious than Orthodox, who always had a runny nose, was always clutching a damp handkerchief, and who always said the prayers in English. And a rabbi from Panama who ran off with stolen money. And one from Mexico who only showed up every now and then, for holidays, and another one, also from Mexico, who used to sweat so much when he was praying that he'd have to change his skullcap halfway through the service. But the vast majority of the rabbis, as I remember it, were from Argentina. One, who was always extolling the virtues of the Boca Juniors soccer team and preaching against mixed marriages, got a local Catholic girl pregnant and later married her (own goal, as my grandfather rather philosophically put it). Another Argentinian, a nice young guy named Carlos, who arrived just in the years when I began to distance myself from Judaism and from my family (you can't do one without the other), used to talk to me about music and nothing else. I'd begun listening to jazz. He also listened to jazz, or he knew about jazz, or maybe he just knew three or four names and used them as a way of bridging the gap. In any case, I was really mixed up at the time. I was very sensitive about everything and very frustrated by everything. I'd recently left home, which also meant leaving behind my father's religion and everything about his glass-house world. And I really appreciated the fact that Carlos, instead of pestering me, would just talk about Armstrong and Coltrane and Parker and Monk. All except for the last time I saw him (he later moved to Israel with his family). It was in the street, in front of a kids' ice-cream parlor. We greeted each other. We chatted a little. I told him what was going on with me, possibly a bit anxiously or unhappily, and so Carlos, out of the blue, asked me if I remembered the story of Abraham. The first Jew, he added, smiling. No, I told him. Well, more or less. Still smiling, he quoted a line from the book of Genesis: Get thee out of thy country, and from thy kindred, and from thy father's house, unto a land that I will show thee. Lech l'cha, he said in Hebrew, with a wink, and that was all.

My grandmother let go of my hand and shifted slightly and the maroon-and-black-checkered quilt also moved a little, and I thought with a fright that I was about to see the face of my dead grandfather.

My grandmother wanted to say something to me, but the words wouldn't come to her, or maybe she didn't know what words to say. I leaned a little closer to her, as though to help. Oh Eduardito, she whispered, and then, with a half-smile, added: That was what your grandfather used to call you, wasn't it? And she repeated the diminutive of my name a couple of times, her jaw trembling, her voice gradually fading, her pale blue eyes sinking floorward again. I considered her face. A sweet lady, my grandmother, very compassionate and good-natured, but overly sentimental as well. She told me once that her father, my great-grandfather, a Jew from Damascus who lost all the family's money at cards, would never allow his children to kiss him except on the hand. Nothing else. Just kiss him on the hand. Never, my grandmother said with an amazing sadness, I never got to embrace my father.

Far off, the growing murmur of visitors could be heard in the dining and living rooms.

The rabbi was talking to my grandmother about Noah and the Flood and a rainbow among the clouds and I began looking around my grandparents' bedroom. There, next to the bed, still hung the only photo my grandfather had managed to keep of his family in Łódź, all of them dead in ghettos or concentration camps: his sisters Raquel (Ula) and Raizel (Rushka), his younger brother Salomón (Zalman), his parents Samuel (tailor) and Masha (washerwoman). Gray, bland faces, all too distant for me. I thought about the last time I'd said to my grandfather that I wanted to travel to Poland, to Łódź, and about his reaction that had bordered on violent. What do you want to go to Poland for? he said. You mustn't go to Poland, he said, but later he jotted down for me on a small piece of yellow paper (as though it were a small inheritance for a grandson, or a key to a long-buried family secret) his address in Łódź, in precise detail: ground floor of the building on the corner of Żeromskiego and Persego Maja, number 16, near the Zielony Rynek market, near Poniatowskiego Park. And I thought about the number tattooed on my grandfather's forearm, 69752, a faded green number that as children he told us was his phone number, and he'd smile, saying he had it tattooed there so he wouldn't forget it. And I thought about Rena Kornreich, another Polish survivor of Auschwitz, who years later, as she herself told it, had her number surgically removed, 1716, but instead of throwing it away, she had kept that small piece of skin, that small piece of herself, in a bottle of formaldehyde. And I thought about Primo Levi, about the number tattooed on Primo Levi's forearm, 174517, and how, whereas my grandfather avoided his number, hid it, made a joke out of it so as not to acknowledge it, and whereas Mrs. Kornreich tore hers off, Primo Levi left instructions for his to be engraved on his tomb. And so there, on a tombstone in the Jewish cemetery in Turin, both his name and his number are engraved: his family name and that other, more sinister name. Both, I suppose, like it or not, intrinsic elements of his identity.

Now the rabbi was talking to my grandmother (who was taking no notice) about some pact of God's (Hashem, he kept saying) after the Flood, and I went on studying my grandparents' bedroom. I noticed three things that were out of place. On my grandfather's bedside table, a candle was burning; the wall mirror above the dresser was covered with an enormous white sheet; the window, always kept shut because of the draft, was wide open. Shlomo had finished his little homily now and I asked him about these three things.

Still standing, he seemed to get a real kick out of being able to explain them to me. Whispering, he said that when a Jew dies, a candle is lit because the flame dispels negative energies; that when a Jew dies, all the mirrors in the house are covered so as to eliminate vanities; that when a Jew dies, a window is opened in the room where his body lies, symbolically, so that, as it says in the Torah, in the Book of Daniel, his body might be aided in its ascent to heaven. Shlomo smiled beneficently and topped it off with a few words in Hebrew and I could have sworn I heard harps. He suddenly came a little closer to me, leaned in a little closer. I thought he was about to tell me something else, something very ceremonious and deeply Jewish. I gritted my teeth. Yesterday, he whispered, I came back from Tikal.

I watched the ice cubes melting languidly on my grandmother's knee.

You've been to Tikal, Shlomo said. I liked Tikal very much, he said, and to assure himself that he had conveyed the full extent of his enthusiasm for the Mayan ruins in the Petén jungle, he repeated it twice: Very much, very much. I said nothing. His enthusiasm, in front of a dead body, seemed out of place. I wanted to get up and tell him so, make my excuses and quietly leave my grandparents' room. But the rabbi placed his warm, furry paw on my shoulder and, very softly, almost breathing the words down at me, began telling me about his trip, about the Mayan temples, about the heat in the jungle, the animals in the jungle, the tourists, about his guide, Juan, a squat, dark-skinned fellow and a terrific guide, he said, a very nice fellow, he said, gripping my shoulder hard, as if to keep me from moving, as if he'd guessed that I wanted to get out of there as soon as possible. Do you know Juan the guide? he asked, and I just smiled as cynically as I could. He was with us the whole day, Juan, and at the end of the day, he asked us if we wanted to see the sunset from one of the temples, I don't remember which, maybe the biggest and tallest one. Shlomo looked up at the ceiling of my grandparents' bedroom, metaphorically. He could take us up there, he said. From up there, he said, we'd have a great view of the sun going down over the jungle canopy.

He was interrupted by the noise of sandals in the corridor. I knew right away that it was Julie, the Salvadorean lady who had been working for twenty years as my grandparents' cook.

Julie came into the bedroom and walked straight over to me. I wanted to get up and hug her, but the weight of something—possibly the rabbi's hand on my shoulder—prevented me. Julie smiled with her gold and silver teeth. We gave each other a sideways hug. Don León is resting at last, she said, and turned toward the maroon-and-black-checkered quilt, and I remembered the last time I had seen my grandfather alive, or at least still with a little life left in him, a few weeks earlier, when I had just gotten back from a long trip to the Balkans (chasing ghosts) and Portugal (tearing realities). I'd come to my grandfather's house to say goodbye, and I knew it was for the last time. He was already very ill. Almost unconscious. Frail and thin, his skin yellowing and flaky. He was delirious. He thought he could see his mother. He thought he was surrounded by German soldiers. My uncles and aunts were having coffee in the dining room, my cousins watching a Spanish league match in the living room. I peered tentatively into the bedroom, and then stood in the doorway watching Julie, who was kneeling on the carpet beside the bed, stroking my grandfather's forehead. I didn't go in. There was no need. I said goodbye to my grandfather for the last time in silence, from the doorway, while I watched Julie on her knees in her white uniform, and listened to the way she whispered to my grandfather. Futile words, pious words, words of encouragement and tenderness.

Julie sat down next to my grandmother on the bed. She took my grandmother's hand. Would you like anything, Doña Matilde? she asked. But my grandmother didn't reply. Doña Matilde, I said would you like anything? With an effort, my grandmother roused herself and said no, nothing, thank you very much. Julie quickly got up. She sighed. I made crabapples in syrup, she said to me, already on her way over to the door, her back to us. She knew how much I liked her crabapples in syrup. I put some in a jar for you, she said. Don't leave without your jar.

My grandmother adjusted the bag of ice on her knee and the rabbi squeezed my shoulder to get my attention. And so, he said, we went up to the temple in Tikal to see the sunset.

I felt something in my belly. Rage, perhaps.

From up there the jungle went on forever, the rabbi whispered, rubbing at his matted beard. The sun was orange, and it was going down, and it was as if it was disappearing into the trees. An incredible sight, he said.

My grandmother began to cough. She covered her mouth with a dirty handkerchief.

There was a Mayan man up there, in the temple, said Shlomo. He was sitting up there. Barefoot. Dark-skinned.

His leather and rubber sandals to one side. He had a pad open on his lap and he was sketching the sunset.

My grandmother carried on coughing quietly into the handkerchief. Shlomo shot her a look, as if to make her shut up.

The man was sketching the sunset, repeated Shlomo, one hand still on my shoulder, the other drawing something invisible in the air. But he sketched it like this, really quickly, said Shlomo, maybe imitating the action. He'd make a very quick sketch with his colored crayons and then he'd tear out that sheet and throw it down on the top of the Mayan temple, on the stones of his ancestors, and he'd begin again, sketching another sunset. Do you understand? Because every sketch was different, every sunset was different, as if there were many sunsets. Everything was changing very quickly. The passage of the clouds, the position of the sun, the color of the sky. Everything. And the man was sketching these changes in a hurry. Capturing them, there on his sheets of paper. He was registering the various moments of a sunset on his sheets of paper, or something like that, said Shlomo. But instead of with a camera, he was doing it with his eyes and his hands and his colored crayons. With his imagination. An incredible sight, he said, excited, so excited that he was no longer speaking in whispers but in a loud, lofty, almost mythic tone. And the Mayan man, the rabbi went on, he just left his sketches strewn across the temple, and the wind started blowing some of them around. As if they didn't matter to him or as if the actual drawings weren't what really mattered. Shlomo leaned in farther still, coming even closer to me. And get this, he said warmly. We tourists, all ten or fifteen of us, virtually forgot about the sunset over the jungle and just stood watching this Mayan man sketching it with his colored crayons. Incredible, isn't it? The artist and his sunset art became more interesting to us than the sunset itself. Shlomo smiled down at me through his grubby red beard. You do understand, right? You must understand.

He paused. People were approaching along the corridor. I took advantage of the pause to remove the rabbi's hand from my shoulder, and he seemed perplexed, offended almost, as I jumped up from the chair.

Two old men came in wearing black jackets, black ties, and black expressions. Two of my grandfather's friends, I guessed. I didn't recognize them, but they seemed to know me and came up and both said how sorry they were, that Don León had been a great man, a great Jew, a great survivor. And as they went on speaking, I thought about the number tattooed on my grandfather's forearm. I thought about the five digits, green, faded, already dying on my grandfather's forearm beneath that thick maroon-and-black quilt. I thought about Auschwitz. I thought about tattoos, about numbers, about sketches, about temples, about sunsets. I thought about telling the two old men they'd gotten it wrong, that first and foremost my grandfather had been a great whiskey drinker, an expert whiskey drinker. But I only murmured yes, he was, thank you, while for the first time I felt like crying and I started backing away from the vague little shape that had been my grandfather and ran out of the room and out of the house, and outside, already a long way from it all, I finally took off the white skullcap and threw it in a garbage can.

About the Author

Eduardo Halfon was born in Guatemala City, moved to the U.S. at the age of ten, went to school in South Florida, studied Industrial Engineering at North Carolina State University, and then returned to Guatemala to teach literature for eight years at Universidad Francisco Marroquín. Named one of best young Latin American writers by the Hay Festival of Bogotá, he is also the recipient of the prestigious José María de Pereda Prize for the Short Novel and has published nine books of fiction in Spanish. In 2011 he received a Guggenheim Fellowship to work on continuing the story of *The Polish Boxer*, which is inspired by his own family history and is the first of his novels to be published in English. Halfon currently lives in Nebraska and travels frequently to Guatemala.

The Translators

Ollie Brock, Thomas Bunstead, Lisa Dillman, Daniel Hahn and Anne McLean have between them worked on 66 books to date, including translations from Spanish, Portuguese, Catalan and French, several of which have won major awards. Rather than compete with one another to introduce Eduardo Halfon's work to an English-speaking readership, they decided to work closely together to produce this collaborative translation of *The Polish Boxer*.

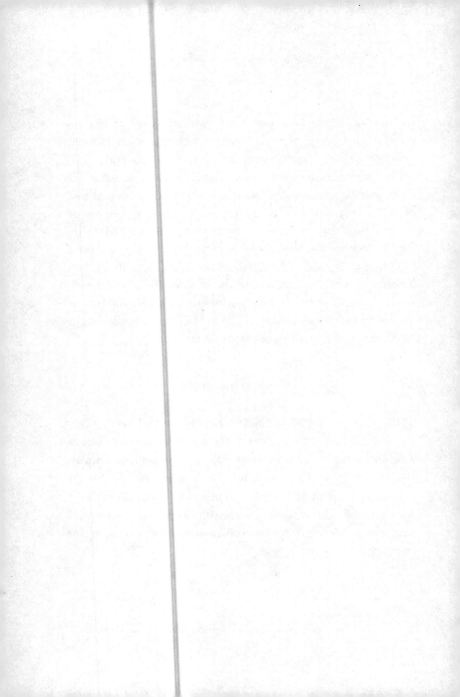